"You have the most perfect lips. When you're thinking, you bite your bottom lip and it drives me crazy," said Cameron.

She trembled at the words, his heated breath spreading across her face. He must be moving closer, must be thinking of all the ways she wanted him to enjoy her mouth.

"When you lick your lips I want it to be me. Hell, even watching you eat turns me on."

The sound of his voice, the scent of him in the warm air of the car, threatened to overload her senses. Dazed by the chemistry flowing between them, Lauren leaned forward until her lips found his. Her hands drifted to his body of their own volition. In his kiss she tasted the wine from dinner, the deep chocolate from the dessert they'd shared, and a desire so electric it melted her inhibitions. He captured her lips, nibbled, sucked with a passion she'd only read about. In an instant she lost all sense of time or place, exchanging kisses that taunted and tempted, diving into a sea of longing that threatened to drown them both.

Jenna Bayley-Burke is a domestic engineer, freelance writer, award-winning recipe developer, romantic novelist, cookbook author and freebie fanatic. Blame it on television, a high-sugar diet, or ADD; she finds life too interesting to commit to one thing. Except her high school sweetheart and two blueberry-eyed baby boys. She hides out in the Pacific Northwest, where it doesn't rain half as much as people think. www.jennabayleyburke.com.

Recent titles by the same author:

JUST ONE SPARK…

COOKING UP
A STORM

BY
JENNA BAYLEY-BURKE

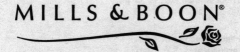

MILLS & BOON®

First published in Great Britain 2006
Harlequin Mills & Boon Limited,
Eton House, 18-24 Paradise Road, Richmond, Surrey TW9 1SR

© Jenna Bayley-Burke 2006

ISBN-13: 978 0 263 85003 1
ISBN-10:   0 263 85003 X

Set in Times Roman 10½ on 12 pt
171-1206-58455

Printed and bound in Spain
by Litografia Rosés, S.A., Barcelona

COOKING UP
A STORM

For Jeff, who continues to keep an open mind about my culinary creations.

CHAPTER ONE

THE gray sky outside his office window mocked him. Cameron Price reminded himself that it was claimed it rained more in New York than here in Seattle, but that little tidbit hadn't kept the leaden sky from unloading its fury each time he stepped outside.

He needed to like it here. Maybe it would help if he focused on the positive. In the summer it would be beautiful, but he had to get through November without going mad. And the coffee tasted better, though he couldn't decipher the way people ordered it. At least he was lucky enough to drive a great car and live in a big house. But the car was a gas-guzzler and the house as white and cold as a hospital.

He sat down in the leather desk chair. He'd driven into the city, to get a vision of his new workplace in its Saturday relaxed attitude. Everyone expected him to show up on Monday, but he wanted to get an idea of the inner workings before he started meeting people at the party tonight.

When he'd arrived, technicians had been setting up the computer and phone in his office. Cameron had toured the building on previous trips to Seattle for meetings, so he knew the layout well enough to find his office. This had allowed him not to look completely out of place standing outside the door, covertly listening as two of his executives had instructed the tech people on the set-up.

From the irritated tone of their voices he knew he had his work cut out for him. The challenge relieved him; he'd been so worried the smaller branch of the venture-capital firm wouldn't give him enough opportunities to prove to the board he could steer the ship.

He'd entered the office with a smile and greeted the two men as if they hadn't been talking behind his back. Cameron was proud of his reputation of efficiency, even if it did mean some people called him ruthless. He made money for the firm and their investors, and that was the bottom line.

They had spoken to him with thinly veiled curiosity, wanting to know his plans for the firm. Of course he'd told them nothing, partly to seem mysterious and authoritative, and partly because he wasn't sure yet just what this promotion entailed, and how much control he'd be allowed to wield. After a brief conversation about the weather, Cameron had ushered them all out of his new office, knowing he'd see them later tonight at Bob Anders' house. Except now it was his house. He had to start thinking of himself as living here, instead of just stepping in and filling the boss's shoes on the West Coast.

When Anders had confessed he hoped to retire in three years, and was looking to Cameron to take over as CEO when he did, Cameron had never expected the honor to include a stint running the West Coast office. A native New Yorker, he'd never expected to live anywhere but the East Coast. But he wanted to helm the most influential venture capital firm in the country as he wanted his next breath, so he'd nodded and smiled, and taken the next plane out.

Two days later, he was struggling to adjust to a new town, new house, and new job. He knew he'd made the right decision, the only decision to make his career aspirations happen. He needed to get his bearings and figure out how everything worked. This fish-out-of-water feeling didn't sit well with him, and he needed to be rid of it quickly.

"The view is better when the mountain is out."

Cameron swiveled in his chair to face the door, seeing his mentor and boss, Bob Anders, framed in the doorway. He smiled at the older man. "The mountain comes in and out?"

"From the clouds." Bob nodded his bald head and entered the room, closing the door behind him. "You'll see. I had to learn to like New York; you'll learn to like Seattle."

"It's always raining, Bob."

"Get used to it, Cam."

They both laughed. "Anything else I should know from someone who grew up here? You owe me. I showed you the best hot dogs, pastrami and bagels New York has to offer."

"That you did. Let's see: never complain about the rain and enjoy the outdoors."

"In the rain?" Cameron's lip curled in a smirk.

"I warned you about that." Bob shook his head and returned the grin. "Everything ready for the party tonight?"

"Should be." Bob's wife Sonja had given him a number and said she'd used the catering company whenever they'd had to entertain in town.

"You'll be doing a lot of this, you know. Entertaining clients, investors, and staff. It's an important part of the leadership role here."

"You mentioned that." And little else.

"It's a lot for one person to take on. That's why Sonja has been so assertive on the wife issue."

Cameron straightened his shoulders. Not this again. "I don't see how that makes any difference. I can hire people to cater and clean; I don't need—"

Bob held up his hand. "You'll see. Listen to Sonja on this one. Besides, she's good at this. We're not talking about finding you some trophy bride. You need a capable, intelligent partner who can handle everything and make your life easier. You have too much to do running this branch of the company and managing your own funds to keep getting tied up with little details. I'll be here Monday for the introductory meeting, and you can always reach me by phone, but I don't expect to have much to do with this office."

"What does that mean?"

"Cam, I'm not as young as I used to be. Ferrying back and forth between both coasts is just too much. And it put a lot of pressure on you to run the New York office. This way, I'll be able to give one hundred percent to New York and not worry about the funds managed here. You have complete authority over the goings on here. Neither I, nor the board, will second-guess your decisions. And in a few years, I'll be able to retire. You can choose which office to run the firm from."

"I appreciate the confidence you have in me."

Bob waved his hand through the air and stood. "There is no better place for you to develop the new alternative energy fund. I stopped in today to make sure things were set up for you, but you've already done that. One step ahead of me, just like in New York."

Cameron stood and followed Bob to the door.

"You should probably head out to the house. Traffic can be murder."

"Are you sure you and Sonja wouldn't be happier at the house than in a hotel? It's not like there isn't room. And you have lived there off and on for a while now."

"Sonja prefers the hotel, closer to shopping and less traffic. Besides, it's your home now."

With a nod Bob left, leaving Cameron alone in the near-empty office. He saw it as if for the first time. The room was a virtual copy of his New York office. Standard mahogany desk and bookshelf, leather desk chair, small round table and three chairs in the corner. Even the same model of telephone. And just as in New York, nothing adorned the walls. He hadn't thought it odd until he'd gone to pack up his office last week, and left with little more than a document box.

He shook his head and shrugged into his coat, making his way out of the offices with a minimum of head nods, thankful the sky spared him as he stepped across the parking lot to the cherry-red Corvette.

Like the house, the car had been Anders'. Cameron found the purr of the engine exciting as he pulled into traffic. He longed for an open road, but instead he got bumper-to-bumper traffic and much too much time to think about the song and dance he'd have to put on at tonight's dinner party.

He didn't enjoy the falseness behind charm and chatter sure to come from tonight's party, employees trying to say what they thought he wanted to hear in order to get on his good side. He preferred honest opinions to groveling. He dreaded the schmoozing, but relished the opportunity to prove to the executives at the Seattle branch of Anders & Norton that he was indeed the man for the job.

Turning up Debussy louder, he let his mind wander to a place he rarely went. So often numbers and facts filled his brain. But this sound system had amazing acoustics for such a small car. The piano suite vibrated through him, so loud and melodious it was almost as if he were playing himself.

He'd played twice a day since he'd arrived. The piano room at the house was a bright light in this whole scheme. He smiled as the music took over, feeling the notes in his fingers and seeing them in Technicolor in his mind. After Debussy came Chopin and softer colors, almost relaxing him. Until he took the exit off the cramped freeway and steered towards suburbia and the house he'd live in for the duration of his time in Seattle.

Cameron drew in a deep breath and clutched the steering wheel tighter as he waited for the garage door to rise. As he tried not to think about the hour and a half he'd wasted in traffic his gaze avoided the digital clock on the dashboard and instead took in the outside of the house. The front of the house was as gray as the Seattle sky, again threatening a cold November rain.

Pulling into the garage, Cameron killed the engine and sighed in resignation. Tonight, the top twenty executives at Anders & Norton would convene on this house to find his weaknesses and exploit them. He'd have to find theirs first.

Never in the history of time did there exist more perfect raspberries. And in the middle of November, no less. As perfect as she needed this party to be, her first for Cameron Price. She knew nothing about the elusive venture capitalist, except he'd left a message instructing her to duplicate the last party she'd catered here at the Anders' house. Last summer, when raspberries had been ripe and plentiful.

Lauren Brody tucked her strawberry blonde hair behind her ears and popped a raspberry in her mouth, instantly remembering why she preferred her fruit in season. The sweet tartness she expected turned out to be more tart than sweet. She swallowed and took a deep breath, the warm scents of toasting potatoes and roasting garlic warming her troubled mind. She smoothed her palms against her white blouse and black trousers, the professional look of the uniform comforting her.

This party would be perfect, she'd see to that. She always did. Come For Dinner catering was known for creating perfect dinner parties for business executives in their homes. That was how she avoided the wedding and engagement party circuit. She shuddered at the thought of having to deal with stressed-out brides every day.

It was much better to work in elegant kitchens like the one in the Anderses' home. Well, Cameron Price's home now, she assumed, since the party served to announce his ascension to managing partner, and running the Seattle office of the venture-capital firm. That was all she'd been able to get out of his assistant. She couldn't get a hold of the man himself to find out if there were any food allergies or special diets she needed to account for, or what his personal tastes were. And still, with so little to go on, she had to create his perfect coming-out party.

Lauren dropped one basket of raspberries into a tall pitcher and covered them with ice-cold vodka. She swirled the mixture and inhaled nothing but the crisp scent of pure alcohol. Not good. She turned and plastered on her most pitiful expression.

"Tell me you brought it." Lauren stuck her lower lip out for good measure. Her chef, Diego Vargas, had been dead set against replicating the raspberry menu.

Diego turned from his chilled avocado soup and shook

his dark head at her. "It's in the green cloth bag. We'll need to line the rest of them up on a sheet pan and spritz them with simple syrup, then let it dry."

"You are a culinary god, and I bow at your greatness." Lauren gave her best curtsey and scampered past Ricky to get to her salvation. A bottle of Chambord, sure to put enough raspberry kick in her pitcher of raspberry martinis. She spun back around to find Ricky had already spread the remaining raspberries, more than enough for the salad and dessert, on a sheet pan per Diego's instructions.

A smile lifted her cheeks as she took in the scene. The granite countertops glistened and pale hardwood floors shone from the cleaning that always began the party preparations. The maple cabinets had a built-in wine rack, but it was empty. Lauren wasn't sure if that meant Price had just moved in, or abstained from alcohol. She prayed it wasn't the latter. She didn't do virgin cocktails.

"I'll go dress the bathroom," Anne, perpetually in charge of cleanliness, said, as she bustled through the kitchen, picking up the box of towels, linens and candles.

"I left an extra vase of roses on the sideboard. Will you place it on the dressing table?" Lauren watched as she nodded and walked out of the kitchen with purpose.

"You went overboard with the roses." Diego's white teeth flashed against his dark skin.

Lauren returned the smile, uncapping the Chambord and pouring in enough to make the martinis delicious. She placed the pitcher into the stainless-steel refrigerator.

"That is one impressive man." Anne returned to the kitchen and set the box down, pretending to faint into one of the kitchen chairs. "I'm talking TDH in a power suit.

And the brightest blue eyes I have ever seen. Iridescent almost. Yummy."

Electric-blue eyes! Oh, dear. This could be a problem. Lauren closed her eyes and took a deep breath, the handsome face of a guest at one of the Anderses' parties two years ago filling her mind. She shook her head to dispel the piercing cerulean gaze making her pulse race.

She hadn't caught his name, or seen him since. But damn it if he didn't have the bluest eyes she'd ever seen. And he'd spiced up her dreams on more than one occasion. Damn, damn, and double damn. She knew better than to ogle random party guests. It would be just her luck if that guest turned into her client.

"What are you talking about?" To keep her hands busy, Lauren started chunking the Brie for the salad, reminding herself no one knew what she'd fantasized about.

Anne crossed to the sink, washing her hands. "I think it's the client, Price, but I didn't ask. I'm telling you, if I were twenty years younger I would have offered to have his children."

"Anne!" Lauren bumped her with her hip. "No propositioning the clients. We're a full-service catering company, but that's one service I draw the line at."

Anne smiled at Ricky and Diego. "He seemed rather pleased with the way Lauren dressed the rooms."

Lauren grinned; glad she'd impressed him. Not because he might be the man she drooled over, but because she needed this account. The Anderses entertained here a few times a year, but they were on the East Coast the rest of the time. If Cameron Price was taking over for him on the west coast, this account had amazing potential. Save them from catering for frantic brides kind of potential.

She finished off the salads, sprinkling yellow pear tomatoes, the cubes of creamy Brie, toasted pine nuts and the sweetened raspberries over the mesclun. She loved this salad; the vibrant colors always impressed. She stored the plates in the bare fridge. There hadn't been a single thing inside it when they'd arrived.

"The potato crisps are done," Lauren said, scrunching her nose as she sniffed the air. "One more minute and they'll be burned. And that charred stench will permeate the house." Lauren turned to face Diego, placing her hands on her hips. Diego continued to be mesmerized by cuddling the giant bowl and whisking his pale green soup..

"Lauren you really should take a peek." Anne leaned a hip against the counter. "He was walking up the stairs, and in all my years I have never seen a more perfect—"

"Hey!" Diego cut in, setting the large bowl on the counter. "If I were talking about a woman that way, you'd all have my head."

Why did everyone have their hormones in a knot? "Fine! I'll take care of the potatoes myself." She marched towards the oven, pulling a towel off the counter to grab the pan with. The corner of the towel must have been under the bowl because it spun out of control and off the counter.

Sounds rushed at her ears. The clatter of the whisk as it flew out of the bowl and bounced against the granite, the thud of the bowl as it jumped onto the hardwood floor, the splat of the soup as it sloshed across her body, dripping down her face, against her starched white shirt and down her pants, where it met the rest of the dish soaking her feet. Everyone froze, staring at her for a second before Diego began barking orders.

"Ricky, take the potatoes out and sprinkle them with

gray salt. Anne, you're on this soup mess." He stepped closer to Lauren and reached out a hand to touch her, but pulled it back, probably to avoid coating himself with avocado. "Do you have another uniform in the car?"

Lauren shook her head, watching everyone bustle around her. "I picked up my dry cleaning on the way here, but—"

"Ricky, go to Lauren's car and grab her dry-cleaning bag." Ricky's curly head disappeared before she could protest. But then, what choice did she have? She stared down at her sensible black loafers, covered in green slime.

"Anne, I don't suppose you have any shoes in your car?"

Cameron had barely unpacked his suitcases, could hardly make it into the office without getting lost, and he already had to put on a performance for the team of people who probably all thought they should've been given his job. Tonight, he was the one on show.

He stood on the landing and leaned over the railing, taking in the view of the downstairs. Come For Dinner catering earned every penny, no matter what they charged him. The house looked better than he'd ever seen it. Sonja Anders had decorated everything in white. Sterile, stark, cold. Now the rooms were washed in warm light, red scarves covering the lampshades and adding to the ambiance.

It was intimate, without being romantic. Classic, without being feminine. Everything he needed it to be. A weight lifted from him as he descended the stairs. He liked that it looked different, not wanting to seem like junior filling in for the boss.

The change in lighting, red pillows and throws on the couches, lush green plants in shiny silver pots, and little vases overflowing with red roses lining the dining room table and scattered on every other open surface made a statement. Saying to all who entered he was here to make his mark on the company.

At the base of the staircase he checked his watch. Ten minutes until the party started; guests would be arriving any minute. He wiped his palms against the gray wool of his trousers and closed his eyes, enjoying the solitude while he could.

A warm force plowed into his chest, opening his eyes with a start. He gripped the whirlwind by her slim shoulders and looked into her large round eyes framed by long blonde eyelashes. He couldn't help but grin at the startled look in that gold-flecked green gaze. Without letting her go, he pulled back, taking in the smattering of freckles crossing her button nose, the long strawberry-blonde hair pulled tight into a braid, and the milky skin of her shoulders, bare but for the thin spaghetti straps of her gauzy black dress. He blinked hard, bringing himself out of shock, and dropped his hands, running one through his hair.

"I'm sorry. I didn't realize anyone had arrived yet." Cameron looked about the room for her date, but saw no one. She looked vaguely familiar, but both of the female executives invited were old enough to be this woman's mother. "Who did you come with?"

An impish grin played on her pouty pink lips. She held out her hand. "I'm Lauren Brody, with Come For Dinner catering."

"Oh. I apologize for assuming." Stupid. Caterers could be pretty and well dressed. "I just never expected…wait, have we met?"

Her head jerked back and she gasped, her hand pressing

against her stomach. Then just as quickly as she reacted, she calmed. "No, we haven't been introduced. But I've catered parties for the Anderses." Her voice was breathy, almost to the point of a whisper.

"Have you decorated this way before?"

"No." She shook her head. "Mrs Anders had her own sense of style. But I assumed since you had so little time to organize the dinner, you wouldn't have time to decorate as well. It's a service we provide for many of our single male clients."

He quirked an eyebrow. "How did you know I was single?" And why did she care?

"I asked your assistant. I needed to know if you would have a date for the evening, for the seating arrangements."

He nodded furiously. Right, seating arrangements. Couldn't just tell people to plop down wherever at a formal dinner. Thank goodness Lauren had him covered on that end. For two years Sonja Anders had been gently encouraging him to get married, but lately her approach had grown more direct. As in blatantly telling him he couldn't handle his new position without a wife. As if he had the time or energy to devote to a relationship.

Sonja Anders was obviously wrong. He didn't need a wife, just Come For Dinner catering.

"If you'd like," Lauren began, "I could give you a run-through of how the night will go." She crossed the room, turning on the stereo and picking up a butane lighter from an end table. Cameron had to smile as the sounds of a jazz group he liked filled the large room.

"Isn't that a little loud?"

"You want it just a smidge too loud at the beginning. Nothing is worse than stepping into a silent house. Gets the social swirl moving. Do you like it? I have blues, classical violin and Etta James if this isn't your style."

"No, this sounds good."

Cameron had liked her before, but with eclectic tastes in music mirroring his own she was dancing in dangerous territory. If he had time, or cared to risk his reputation with trying a relationship, she'd be an option. But showing his vulnerability to the world was not.

"I'll turn it down as we start serving cocktails. Raspberry martinis, and, of course, Chivas for Mr Anders. We'll be serving potato crisps with a caviar dip." She slid about the room lighting candles. Did she know he needed to romance the team into trusting him?

"For dinner I'll lower the volume more while we enjoy salad, and beef filet. I'll turn it up again later on when I serve a flourless chocolate cake with raspberries for dessert."

He watched as she walked around the room as if she owned the place, far more comfortable there than he was. But then, she knew how to throw a party. He was less experienced. He could convince people to invest millions in a groundbreaking idea with nothing more than his word, but he had no idea how to get those same people to enjoy a party.

"Thank you for putting all of this together tonight. It's exactly what I needed."

A gleaming smile lit her face, lifting her rosy cheeks. "I'm glad to hear that. I hope—"

The shrill peal of the phone interrupted her. Cameron held up a finger so she would hold that thought and stepped to the side table, lifting the receiver. Before he got out so much as a hello, the doorbell chimed.

CHAPTER TWO

LAUREN scampered to the door, grateful for the chance to catch her breath. She'd tried to focus on work while talking to Cameron Price, but she kept getting distracted by his bright blue eyes, fringed with unfairly long dark lashes. And that voice. A rich baritone, filled with lascivious suggestion.

She pulled open the front door. Bob and Sonja Anders stood at the entry and she stepped aside, waving them in. Sonja arched a perfectly shaped blonde brow and eyed Lauren as she entered the foyer.

Looking down at her feet, Lauren winced. Barefoot. Great way to impress a woman like Sonja Anders, shod in expensive designer shoes.

"Can I take your coats?" Lauren offered, looking for any chance to slip away. In seconds Sonja would be commenting on Lauren's lack of uniform and footwear, which might mean she'd have to explain about the unfortunate avocado incident. Best to disappear rather than let a client know something had gone wrong.

"Bob can hang them in the closet." Sonja shrugged out of her ivory sheared mink coat to reveal an elegant off-white boucle dress suit. "Did you bring extra hangers down?"

Lauren nodded and wished she hadn't doused herself in avocado. In her work uniform she knew her place. Her perfect little black dress usually made her feel confident and sexy, but next to Sonja Anders' obvious couture the black viscose silk dress felt off season. And being three years old, it was.

"This is very interesting," Sonja said as Bob retreated with their coats. "I had no idea. I should have thought of it. You are the perfect solution."

"Am I?" Lauren smiled, lost and desperately needing a translation. Was Sonja commenting on the slight changes in décor?

"You know, it makes perfect sense."

Lauren's eyes widened in confusion. Sonja smiled and patted her arm.

"Sorry about that." Cameron said, joining them and standing beside her. Lauren was glad for the reprieve from Sonja's confusing scrutiny.

"I'm going to go check on dinner. It was nice seeing you again." She smiled at Sonja and tried to retreat to the less-puzzling confines of the kitchen, but Cameron's warm fingers on her arm stalled her.

"Thank you, Lauren. For everything." Oh, that smile could be lethal. Absolutely deadly. Lauren nodded and prayed he used his powers for good rather than evil.

"There are quite a few women who will be very disappointed." Sonja Anders' voice lilted as she shook her head and smiled, her perfectly coifed blonde hair not moving an inch.

"How so?" Never sure what to make of her, Cameron tried to remain noncommittal and hoped Bob would come back from the coat closet soon.

"You know, Cameron, you could have told me you were seeing someone, saved me the trouble of compiling a list of potential women for you. But then—" she laid a hand on his arm, the blood-red manicured fingernails bright against the dark gray of his shirt "—this is new, isn't it? I'll keep the list, just in case."

Damn. Sonja thought he and Lauren were together. He swallowed hard at the idea of Sonja Anders trying to set him up. He had no time for dating, and even if he did care to he couldn't risk it, not with so much on the line.

"What's this?" Bob Anders asked, joining the group.

"Cameron is seeing Lauren Brody," Sonja supplied.

"Who's that?" Bob scrunched his round face.

"The caterer."

"Oh. Good choice. But a bit quick, Cameron."

"I agree. If she doesn't work out, he can start with a few of my suggestions."

Cameron cleared his throat. "I'm not taking suggestions." The Anderses had been parental with him since Bob invited him to join the firm five years ago, but this was over the line.

"Cameron, don't start this again." Sonja pursed her lips and crossed her arms across her chest. "You need someone to help you manage your life. You don't understand the difficulty of the position you are taking on. The paycheck may only have your name on it, but it is a partnership. You need someone to manage the house, coordinate when you entertain, and be your eyes and ears at events. You can't do this alone."

"I'm not. I have Lauren." Cameron understood why Sonja would be so sensitive about this, thinking he needed a wife the way Bob needed her. But he wasn't about to go on dates to validate her sense of self-worth.

"For now." Bob nodded. "And she is a great short term solution, but if things sour you'll be without a companion and a caterer. You should take out a few of Sonja's choices, so you have options."

"No." Cameron shook his head and sighed. How did he make this stop without creating tension with the Anderses? The last thing he needed was people thinking he and Anders had a rift.

"It can't be that serious with her already. You just got here," said Sonja.

"She's been catering your parties for years." *Stop. Stop now.* "Parties I attended, Sonja." *What are you doing?*

"Oh." Sonja stood up straighter. "My. Well, that certainly makes more sense now."

"Good." Glad it did to someone.

"So that's why you never brought a date with you to parties in New York." Bob's cheery grin spread across his face. "You sly devil, you had a girlfriend back here all along. No wonder you agreed so quickly to the move. I thought I'd have to sell you on it, but you jumped at the chance. I'm glad things are so serious."

Cameron opened his mouth, but didn't know what to say. He'd only meant to make Sonja and Bob stop their badgering, not lie his way into a long-term relationship.

Thankfully the doorbell rang again, saving him from having to explain. Though, maybe he wouldn't have to explain tonight. If he could just make it through this party, he could sort the rest out later.

"Would you mind getting that?" he asked Bob. "I want to see what's keeping Lauren."

Cameron dashed off without waiting for a response, needing to see if she'd be at all willing to play along for a night. He headed down the hallway to the kitchen he hadn't so much as stepped into yet and knocked on the door before entering.

Everyone turned to look at him but Lauren spoke first. "Mr Price, can I help you with something?"

He waited for her gaze to lock with his. "You can call me Cameron." He smiled as the kitchen came to life again around them. "Can I talk to you for a moment, privately?"

"Absolutely." She nodded, and then turned to her staff. "Diego, can you make sure the hors d'oeuvres get started?"

The brooding hulk lifted an eyebrow, to which Lauren shrugged her shoulders and shook her head. With a shrug of his own, he turned back around. Cameron's stomach sank. He'd noticed she wore no ring, but hadn't thought far enough ahead to realize a boyfriend might be in the picture. But then, he hadn't done any thinking ahead where this plan was concerned. The doorbell gonged through the house, making Cameron wonder how loud it would seem first thing in the morning. There had to be a way to turn it down.

He ushered Lauren out of the kitchen and into the hallway, turning them both into the den at the end of the hall. She looked up at him expectantly.

"I've done a really stupid thing," Cameron began, taking a deep breath before digging his hole any deeper. He needed to know one thing about her before he tried to convince her of anything. "You and the big guy in the kitchen—are you together?"

"Big guy? You mean Diego? He's not any taller than you." Her rosy cheeks lifted in a smile. "Why would you think that?"

"Non-verbal communication. Speaks volumes about

relationships." And if she were in one, he wouldn't even bother asking for this favor.

"Ah. We can do that because we often need to talk in front of clients. Like in the kitchen. He wanted to know if I knew what was wrong."

"But outside of work, are you together?"

"Cameron, are you asking if I am single?" She cocked her head to the side, her long braid dangling over her shoulder.

"In a way, yes."

"Diego and I are friends, good friends, but no sparks."

"Good. Because I need a favor, a really big one for this party to run smoothly."

"I'm your girl. Tell me what you need."

Her dusky whisper could be his undoing. Still he had no other option until he could get Anders to see reason on the wife issue. Cameron swallowed his pride.

"I need you."

Lauren's breath caught in her throat and she could have sworn her heart stopped for a full three seconds. "You need me?"

"You've worked for Sonja Anders before, right? You know how…" he pressed his lips together and pondered the ceiling as if looking for the right word to describe the force of nature that was Mrs Anders. "…how determined she can be."

"Yes, I've noticed." Lauren grinned and stared up at him. His eyes had a glassy shine to them, making them even more dynamic.

"Sonja's decided I need a wife—or a girlfriend at least." He shook his head as if he couldn't believe this was happening. That made two of them. "But with this new promotion, the move, and starting the alternative-energy fund,

I don't have the time or energy to devote to a relationship, even if I wanted one."

"Which you don't. Want a relationship, I mean." Too bad.

"Not now, no. But I really don't want to get into an argument with her tonight. If the guests' first impression of me is that I'm feuding with the Anderses, it will be an uphill battle to win their trust."

"And how do I factor into this?"

Cameron rubbed the back of his neck. "I need you to pretend we're together."

Lauren blinked, positive her heart really did stop this time. "Come again?"

"Just for tonight. I'll set Anders straight tomorrow when his wife isn't in tow. Help me get through the evening, and I'll…I'll…"

"You'll what?" She bit her lip, wondering what he might offer.

"I'm trying to think of something you would want. I don't know you very well. Offering you money seems insulting—"

"It is."

"I know." He winced, his naturally down-turned mouth forming a frown. "There has to be something you want from me. Anything."

Lauren bit her cheek to try and dislodge the erotic image dancing before her eyes. That was nothing but the fast track to disappointment. He didn't do relationships, and she didn't have sex outside of them. But she never turned her back on the opportunity to have a little fun, either.

"I understand this is crazy, Lauren. If it weren't my introduction to the firm, I wouldn't be asking. Usually, I set them straight the second they start in, but they assumed something was going on before I could explain, and I need tonight to go well."

Lauren looked him over again. His hair was expertly cut, a little too short, but stylish. The long straight nose, prominent high cheekbones and chiseled chin set an almost arrogant tone to his expression. His skin had a warm glow. The clothes he wore were expensive, tailored, and classic. His shoes Italian, probably handmade. She couldn't understand why he would have trouble finding a girlfriend.

"Why not simply ask someone out?"

"Because—" Cameron took a deep breath and huffed it out "—you ask a woman to do things for you, and she expects you to reciprocate. I don't have time for that. I can't be focused on my job, and give a new relationship what it deserves. Using a woman for her party skills could end badly if she thought there was more to it. This is convenient because you are a caterer, and business, so no disappointments."

Lauren couldn't help but smile. She'd been in the situation he described too many times. Had romantic opportunities fall by the wayside because she'd been too busy trying to get Come For Dinner off the ground. She'd disappointed a few men along the way. At least he knew better than to waste someone's time.

She'd catch hell for this from her friends, but part of her wanted to feel what her parties were like from the other side. And what could it hurt, really?

"An exclusive agreement."

"Excuse me?"

"That's what I want from you. If you, or Anders & Norton, throw a party, Come For Dinner gets to cater it. For, let's say, the next three months."

"Done. You make sure all my parties are as well set up

as this one, and I'll make sure you have as much business as you can handle."

Damn. She should have asked for six months. "Well, okay, then." She offered her hand. He took it with a smile, his firm handshake making her tingle from fingertips to shoulder.

"Sonja thought it was too soon for us to be serious enough for her to call off her wife hunt, so I led her to believe we met a while back at one of their parties."

"A bi-coastal relationship. Interesting." Lauren smoothed her hands against the skirt of her dress and looked down at her feet. "Oh, no."

"What?"

"I don't have any shoes. I can't go out there barefoot."

"What happened to your shoes?" Cameron tilted his head to the side.

"An unfortunate incident with the soup. Hence the dress." What could she do? She'd seen the guest list for this party. Half the crowd were also her clients. She couldn't serve them dinner with her rainy-day red toenail polish on display.

"I'm not following you."

"Picture an avocado facial for my uniform and my shoes. I picked up my dry cleaning this afternoon on my way here and this dress was in the bag. Lucky thing, or else I'd be in the kitchen in my gym clothes."

"So, tell everyone you spilled soup on them."

"I can't. No kitchen disasters can ever overshadow a party." The doorbell chimed again, making them both tense. "We'll tell them I broke a heel, and had no time to go home and get a new pair."

"Brilliant. Let's go."

Lauren swallowed hard. Diego had been after her for months to run a party on his own. And she trusted him. Well, she could trust him. Except with avocado soup. Everything was planned from start to finish. He could do this, if she could only let go.

"I'll clue the kitchen in on what's going on and then be right out."

"You can't tell them." He shook his head frantically.

"I have to tell them something, Cameron. Go, greet your guests, have a drink. I'll be right there."

"Thank you, Lauren."

"Please." She waved her hand through the air. "There are a hundred women who'd have dinner with you for free."

"Maybe, but they'd expect me to call the next day."

"Oh, you'll call. Exclusivity for three months, remember?"

He smiled and turned, and she watched those long legs stride confidently down the hall. Still unsure what her cover story would be to her team, Lauren returned to the kitchen. Diego eyed her as he whisked the vinaigrette. She stepped to him, keeping her shoulders back and her chin up.

"Diego, I need for you to run the dinner tonight."

"You feeling all right?"

"Yes. Cameron has asked me to join him for dinner." She ignored the eyebrow Diego arched and turned to the team, all staring at her wide-eyed. "Anne, can you please arrange another place setting at the table? Ricky, I need you to mock up another salad."

"Hey, I'm running things." Diego nudged her with his muscled arm. "Go, enjoy your date with Mr TDH. What does that mean anyway?"

"Tall, dark and handsome," Anne filled in.

Diego shook his head. "I've got this covered."

She stuck out her tongue at him as she exited the kitchen. Let them think it was a date. They'd all teased her for not dating enough anyway. For a few hours of her time, she'd see a party from the other side of the kitchen, land a fat new account and get her friends off her back for a few months. All for honeying up to Cameron Price.

"Nobody is talking." Standing at the wet bar across from the dining room, Cameron handed Lauren a martini as bright red as her toenail polish and picked up his scotch. His second of the night. He hoped it might calm his nerves, but tension ate at him.

"Yes, everyone does seem to be rather socially stunted." She stretched her neck from one side to the other and took a sip of her drink. "Is this usually how it works? You stare at each other and nod?"

"Usually there is business to discuss. But this is just everyone looking at me." He looked over at the living room where everyone congregated. They all stood expectantly, as if he were supposed to put on a show.

"Well, then it's time you flexed your flirt muscle a bit." Lauren leaned closer as she spoke, her finger running up and down his arm. "You want them to like you. Court them."

"I want them to respect me."

"Sure, but that will come later. Now, you need to proactively impress these people."

"I don't do that."

"Then you need to learn how, sugar. I know just the thing." Lauren linked her arm in his and led him into the room.

His lips curled in distaste, but he followed her anyway. What conversation there was halted as they entered the room. His gaze cut from side to side, recognizing few of the faces. Plastering on the mask of confidence he'd perfected, Cameron greeted his guests and introduced Lauren.

"You know what might be fun?" Lauren slipped away from him and perched on the arm of the couch. "You're all here to get to know Cameron, so how about if everyone asks him a question?"

"You mean like how he takes his coffee?" the woman seated next to her asked. "Or should we be asking you?"

"Cream, no sugar," Cameron supplied to the woman, who looked as if she'd lost a fight with the cosmetics counter.

Lauren sighed and winked at him, crossing her shapely legs and leaning towards the catty woman. "I'm working on that. He has no idea what good coffee is."

The crowd laughed and Cameron felt a bit of the tension ease. His favorite book, Dickens' *Great Expectations,* drew a few nods. As did his growing up in New York City. Lauren played her role so well even he had to remind himself her coy glances and furtive touches were an act.

When someone asked about his education he formed some camaraderie with the controller who, like him, had earned her undergraduate degree at NYU. When he spoke of his time earning his MBA at Harvard, two of the account managers warmed to him in a sense of brotherhood.

At some point Lauren snuck away, but he didn't notice until she slipped a fresh drink into his hand and suggested they all sit down to dinner. Which he probably should have been the one to do. Maybe Lauren would give him some tips on how to host a dinner party.

She did a wonderful job of it. Dinner table conversation flowed like a history lesson of Seattle. They discussed all the happenings of the city—buildings, politics, sports, environmental concerns and cultural events. He learned more than he had on the Internet, and actually got a lead on where he might find a decent bagel, instead of the fluffy white bread thing the girl at the coffee shop had tried to pass off this morning.

When people suggested restaurants for him and Lauren to try she didn't bat an eye, listing places she planned to show him now that they had more time together. The look she gave him across the table convinced him their relationship smoldered with passion, and he knew it was an act. She made the relationship seem as serious and genuine as the Anderses hoped. He'd need more than an exclusive catering contract to thank her for this.

Dessert was fabulous. A dense chocolate slice of heaven that was more fudge than cake. It was the only thing he ate. He'd spent the other courses chatting up someone at the table, it wasn't until dessert that he'd spoken to them all.

After dessert, Lauren ushered everyone into the living room. A waiter arrived with a tray of champagne flutes, red raspberries bubbling at the bottom of every glass.

She'd tied everything together. Raspberries in the martinis, salad, dessert, and now the champagne. No wonder Sonja had recommended her so highly. Lauren was a wonder.

Handing him a flute, she smiled up at him, lacing their hands together and standing much too close. Cameron smiled and looked away, needing to remind himself of the situation.

All he really needed from the girlfriend the Anderses insisted on was a caterer who liked to throw great parties. Maybe she'd be willing to help him again. She'd make sure his parties went off without a hitch, and he'd make sure she had more business than she could handle. Easy enough.

"Cameron," Bob Anders asked. "If I may?" Anders raised his glass and Cameron nodded and smiled, thankful for the save.

"I think we should all raise our glasses to the lady of the evening. Lauren, you've done a wonderful job with the dinner, like always. But more than that, the house looks beautiful, and you've filled in a missing piece of the puzzle for me. Let's all toast to Cameron and Lauren, and their long-distance relationship becoming more permanent now that they live in the same town."

CHAPTER THREE

"I COULD never be in a relationship with someone who didn't ask first." Lauren kept her voice low enough so the guests couldn't hear, but she knew Cameron had by the way he flinched. She beamed up at him as if the announcement pleased her, but she laced her whisper with venom. Being in on a charade for a night was one thing, being played for a fool and tricked into playing the part long term, quite another. Whatever game he wanted to play, it was past time she cashed in her chips.

"Lauren, I—"

She placed her palm against his chest and stood on her tiptoes, placing a kiss against his cheek so she could whisper in his ear. "You need to thank your guests. I need to go finish my job."

With a smile, Lauren excused herself from the well-wishers and their questions, and retreated to the kitchen. She'd indulged her fantasy all evening, only to have her harmless night as Cameron Price's girlfriend turn into a public announcement. Not that she would mind seeing more of Cameron, but she didn't like the assumption. She needed to think her way out of this scrape.

The second she walked in the kitchen door, she wished she had just left the property entirely.

"Congratulations," Anne cackled. From the glowering look on Diego's face, Lauren knew news of her "relationship" had already made it back to her crew. "When's the wedding?"

"I'm not sure, but we're not catering it." Wedding indeed.

"Lauren?" Diego's quizzical expression asked volumes of questions she didn't have answers to. They'd been friends since the first day she'd tried her hand at culinary school. He knew her too well to even try to lie. So she simply looked away, helping to pack the dishes back in the boxes for the rental company.

"Come on, Lauren. How long have you been seeing him? You acted like you'd never met him. Spill a little," Anne said with a nudge against her shoulder.

"I already spilled a lot. Avocado soup, remember?" She closed the lid on the box and looked about the kitchen. It was as clean as if she'd run the dinner herself. "If someone wants to grab my gym shoes out of my car, I'll help load the van."

"Ricky, get the shoes. The rest of you take a load to the van. No one comes back inside for two minutes. *Vamanos*." Diego waved his hands through the air, but his eyes locked with Lauren's, not breaking contact as the crew scurried about.

When the door closed Lauren took a deep breath. "You did a great job running the dinner tonight. Thank you."

"Are you okay with what happened?"

"Absolutely. You've been telling me for a year you could run a job on your own. Now that I know you can, we'll be able to double book small parties."

"I mean with Price." He leaned closer, narrowing his eyes. "What the hell?"

"It's fine, Diego." She smiled, forcing her cheeks to look high and happy. "Seriously, it's not what it seems."

"I guessed that much. So what is it?"

"Besides being none of your business?" Lauren gave him her most impish grin, but it didn't crack his serious façade. "Would you believe I'm going for a gold medal in the dating Olympics? Hello to commitment in less than a day?" Still nothing. Boy needed to buy a sense of humor. "Don't worry about it. I have it under control." As if.

"You sure? Because if you need me to—"

"Diego, honestly. Things are fine. I'm okay, the party went great, and two of the guests tonight said they'd call for their next event. The whole night is a big success."

"Including your relationship with a complete stranger?" He shook his head and tried to hide his chuckle. Didn't work.

"I could never be with someone who doesn't eat. I swear, I think he had two bites all evening." Though he didn't hold back from the scotch and wine. The scotch had seemed to help loosen his tongue, so she'd kept his drink full.

"Yes, a man's appetite is always high on your list." Diego shook his head and leaned against the spotless counter. "I don't want to see you hurt, Lauren."

She held up her hand. "Really, I'm fine."

"Okay. I have to trust you on this. But don't do something crazy like tell Nyla and Christa. They'll have you actually marrying him."

Lauren laughed so hard she snorted at the mere idea of what her best friends would say about the evening's events. They'd both applaud her decision to play the role for the night, but how would they react to realizing the favor for a cute guy she'd agreed to was really a devious plot? Or was it? Maybe Cameron had been unpleasantly surprised as well.

Damn. She had to stop making excuses for him. He wasn't her boyfriend, just a soon to be frequent employer on whom she had a terrible crush. She pursed her lips. That wasn't any better.

"Nyla would only want me to marry him to get to plan the wedding. She's always looking for fresh meat. Like you." Lauren winked, glad to get to goad Diego a bit.

"Don't start."

"You might like it," Lauren teased as the team returned.

"You're the one who is glutton for punishment, not me." Diego shouldered a large box and carried it out to the van.

"Don't let him be too hard on you. He's just mad he had to work tonight and you got to play." Anne loaded her arms with canvas bags that had contained tonight's groceries.

Lauren laughed again, taking the sneakers Ricky offered and sitting at the kitchen table to slip them on.

"You know, honey, I think you have this Cinderella thing backwards. You're supposed to lose a shoe and have him come looking for you. Not go barefoot and slip into running shoes so you can make a getaway."

"Cinderella I'll never be." Lauren stood and looked about the now bare kitchen. "You're all too efficient for me to slave away."

"The only things left are the towels in the bathroom, and the plants, pillows and throws. Since I saw most of the guests driving away, I think it's safe to undress the rooms now," Ricky said, heading for the hallway. Lauren placed a hand on his arm to stall him.

"I'll get that. Why don't you guys head home? You did a wonderful job tonight."

"Oh, I get it," Ricky said with a grin. "She's going to

be doing the undressing herself." He winked and Lauren tried not to laugh.

"Scoot, all of you." Lauren fluttered her hands, ushering everyone out the side door.

The last one out, Diego stopped in the doorway. "I'll stay, if you need me to."

"I told you, I'm fine." Lauren shook her head. She needed to be alone and figure out what to say to Cameron Price, not deal with lectures from her surrogate big brother. "Besides, you have to take Anne home. I'll see you all tomorrow to prep for the Nelson bridal lunch."

She nearly gagged as she waved goodbye to her crew. Cucumber sandwiches for thirty, and petits fours. Jeannie Nelson had ordered the same menu for each of her three daughters' bridal luncheons, even though the last two times she'd claimed Lauren had ruined the event.

In spite of having a wedding planner for a best friend, Lauren hated everything about weddings. The formality, the fighting, the tension. Why the world hadn't collectively decided to elope, she didn't know.

With a deep sigh she closed the door and decided to rescue her plants. Remembering how stark the Anderses' home had always seemed, Lauren had brought all of the plants from her apartment to add some life to the place.

It had worked. The party tonight had been livelier than any she'd ever seen here. It had felt so natural, chatting to the guests. Even the way she'd been able to touch Cameron, flirt, play out an entire seduction scenario in her mind. Not that she'd be able to act it out, but still. She'd embraced the role he'd asked her to play. Embraced it, and enjoyed it.

She'd occasionally indulged in him as a fantasy over the last two years, never thinking she'd see him again. But as soon as she had, the fizzy tingling feeling she'd felt the first time had bubbled through her.

That strange feeling had had her agreeing to play his girlfriend for the evening, and relishing every moment of it. It unnerved her, how easily she'd slid into playing the perfect professional's partner. She'd been bred for it, groomed by her mother to fill the role, but she'd fought it with every ounce of her being until tonight.

Always insisting on being her own woman, she'd been told by the last guy she'd dated she was too independent to be successful at a relationship. And yet tonight, she'd played the part to a tee. Maybe because it had only been temporary, or because she'd been able to schmooze with potential clients at the same time, but whatever it had been had left her feeling mighty confused.

Quiet stillness flooded the darkened house as she walked the rooms, collecting the plant pots two at a time and carrying them out to her Jeep Cherokee. When she had them all snugly lined up in the cargo space, she returned to the house and looked around. She liked the room better with the ruby-red chenille throws and textured crimson pillows. Maybe Cameron would want to keep them.

Lauren let out a tired sigh and retreated to the kitchen. No telling what Cameron was waiting for. If he thought she'd leave before they had a chance to get their stories straight, he had another think coming.

Cameron's entire world felt fuzzy and light as he stripped off his clothes. He didn't feel drunk, really. More loose and relaxed. Except for the breathless, anticipatory feeling that came over him whenever he thought about Lauren.

He collapsed back onto the enormous bed and closed

his eyes. He tried to play out in his head how he'd explain the situation to Anders. They'd backed him into a corner, and he'd improvised. But when they knew the truth, would they just start in on the marriage bit again?

He sure hoped not. Too much work needed his attention to try and have a relationship. Lauren didn't help matters. A superstar of a woman, she'd got the attention of every man in the room tonight. Barefoot and make-up free, no less. If the woman ever turned it on, she'd be irresistible. To him, and to every man who wanted something from him in business. Ruthless men who would be more than willing to use his weakness for her against him if he ever let it show.

He'd carefully kept his weaknesses hidden. Hell, there were probably people back in New York who'd swear he didn't have any. But never before had he been pressured on one side and tempted on the other. He groaned and hoped it was the alcohol making him think of Lauren as more than his caterer.

She'd done him a favor by agreeing to masquerade as his girlfriend for the party, and after she'd played the part perfectly he'd allowed Anders to manipulate the situation into more than it was, after he'd asked her not to tell her staff what was going on. Damn. He'd be lucky if she agreed to speak with him. Continuing the charade on any terms would be out of the question.

Still, he couldn't recall ever having a better night. Good music, great scotch, effortless conversation, and a pretty woman on his arm all evening long. He'd been smart to make the move to Seattle. Something like this would never have happened if he'd stayed in New York.

Stretching against the smooth white cotton of the comforter, Cameron opened his tired eyes and stared at the ceiling. He probably should eat something so he wasn't ravenous before he went for his morning run. He never ate much at these dinners, but usually he didn't drink much either. Pushing up on the bed, he slid his feet to the floor and made his way downstairs.

Painful quiet filled the rooms. So used to the bustle and background noise of New York, he found the stillness un-nerving. Looking about the rooms, he saw that Lauren had left the flowers and the splashes of red in the living room. Maybe she'd let him keep the throws and pillows. They certainly brightened up the space.

He trudged on to the kitchen, hoping the catering crew had left him some bread. Or maybe some cake.

The door made no sound as he pushed it open. Stepping onto the cold tile, he froze. His breath caught and he became agonizingly aware he wore nothing but his black cotton boxer briefs. Underwear that had no hope of hiding his reaction to the fiery woman with her back to him as she shimmied, cleaning something off the counter with a towel.

Really, he should clear his throat and let her know he was there. Or run. Yes, running would be good. Straight upstairs where he could put on some clothes.

Before he could escape she turned, her eyes widening in surprise. Maybe the celebratory toasts had had more of an effect than he realized, because his anxiety vanished and he started to laugh.

"I thought you'd gone home." He crossed the kitchen and stood next to her at the counter. "Since you could never be in a relationship with me and all."

"Cameron—" she turned to face him, but from the tremble in her lips he knew she suppressed a smile "—this isn't a joke. Playing a role for one night is one thing, but a relationship is another."

"Oh, I don't think Anders was joking. He's probably contracting someone to draw up our prenup right now, just to ensure every party I throw is as good as this one. You did a wonderful job."

"I could never marry someone who thinks marriage requires an escape hatch."

"What?" Cameron laughed again. She certainly had a fresh way of phrasing everything. With a smile, he started looking about the kitchen for some sign of sustenance.

"A prenuptial agreement. I'll never sign one, or marry someone who's not fully committed to making a marriage work." She stood taller, pulling her creamy shoulders back.

"Before you get too indignant about it, I have to have one. It's part of my employment agreement so divorces don't affect the other partners." He stepped closer, and then closer than he knew he should. She'd had her hands on him all evening. Had it been just for show, or could there be more to it? "But then that's not really the issue here."

"What are you doing?" Her bottom lip trembled in a completely different way.

"I'm not sure yet."

Lauren's breath caught in her throat as she stared into his darkening blue eyes. Oh, no, he was going to kiss her. And heaven help her, in spite of everything, she wanted him to. Had since before he'd walked into the kitchen without a shirt on. Or pants, for that matter. Not that she'd allowed herself a peek south of the border.

"Are there any leftovers?"

Caught off guard, Lauren blinked, and then shook her head. Of course he wasn't going to kiss her. She was the one with naughty thoughts. Which had to stop right now, so she could focus on finding out what was going on.

Stepping around him, she pulled open the refrigerator and took out the plastic containers, setting them on the counter.

"I'm not sure if there's anything you're willing to eat. You certainly didn't touch your food at dinner."

"That's because I was busy working and everything required too much attention to eat without looking."

She leveled her gaze at him. "If you would have returned my calls, I could have planned a menu you would eat. At a get-to-know-you dinner you should serve your favorite foods."

"Yeah. Macaroni and cheese would have been a big hit with that crowd." He grabbed for the bag containing the eight-grain rolls and pulled one out.

"You eat food from a box?" She shook her head, watching as he ripped the roll in half and shoved in a slice of the beef tenderloin.

"Pretty much. I don't have much time for preparing meals."

Poor baby. She could help him. Expand his palate. "You should try a little of the Gorgonzola sauce to moisten the bread."

Cameron wrinkled his straight nose and set down his impromptu sandwich. "Make it for me."

"Fine." Spinning around, she grabbed one of the ridiculous butter knives from the drawer, then turned back to prepare the best damned sandwich Cameron Price had ever had. Eight-grain roll, Gorgonzola sauce, spinach leaves and marinated onions from the salad. "What would you like me to serve at the next dinner? I don't want to serve another meal you push around the plate."

He chomped into the roll. "I like simple food, so the focus is the meeting and not the eating."

He had to be kidding. "You want me to make food no one will notice."

"Exactly. Potatoes are okay. But not those." He pointed at the plastic container with the roasted potatoes. "They have rosemary on them, so people might worry about getting it in their teeth."

"I could never be with someone who thinks food should be invisible and tasteless."

"Do you want to be with me, Lauren?" Cameron reached around her, pulling a bottle of water out of the fridge. "Is that why you're making a list of ways I'd have to change?" He drained the bottle, his Adam's apple undulating with every heavy second. He set down the empty bottle and his lip curled in a grin. "Well?"

"I'm just saying—" Lauren took a deep breath, trying to sound light and nonchalant "—people who know me would never believe I'd be with someone who refused to eat what I prepare."

"But does it matter? If I'm going to explain everything anyway?" He tilted his head to the side. Earlier his hair had been perfectly combed, but now it flopped onto his forehead, accenting his heavy-lidded eyes. Bedroom eyes, really.

"Here's the thing." She pasted on a smile, wishing she weren't deeply distracted by his nearly naked body. "I think we should break up."

He laughed so hard he fell against the counter, the muscles of his toned stomach rippling as he hunched over.

"Cameron! I'm serious here." To keep from looking at him Lauren shoved the leftovers back into the refrigerator and slammed the door.

"I could never break up with a woman I'm only pretending to see."

Lauren waved her hand through the air. "I don't want people to know we lied. I cater for these people. I don't need them looking down their noses at me for playing this game with you. So, I think instead of coming clean, we should break up."

His sculpted shoulders rose and fell. He might eat badly, but he certainly took good care of the rest of himself. "You may have a point there. Actually, I could use that." He rubbed his finger and thumb against his jaw. "We could go two ways with this. Either I work too much and ignore you, or you work too much and I need someone more dedicated to me."

More dedicated, indeed. "Let's have you ignore me."

"Impossible." He grinned and stepped closer, again standing close enough so she could catch a whiff of his scent, a mixture of clean soap and crisp cologne. "You're just trying to be the one who breaks up with me."

Don't look down. He stood so close if she looked down she'd catch a view that might make her rethink this whole plan. Lauren closed her eyes and took a deep cleansing breath. No good, since the smell of his hard maleness saturated the air.

He stepped closer still, his body touching hers in all the right places. Wrong places. Not right, wrong. Lauren opened her eyes and asked the only question that mattered.

"What kind of game are you playing, Cameron?" She pulled her bottom lip between her teeth, resisting the impulse to wrap her arms around his neck and give into the baser urges coursing through her traitorous body. "How far do you plan on taking this?"

His warm hands wrapped around her upper arms,

hauling her body against his. Before she could remind herself good girls didn't, his mouth was on hers, reminding her instead of two years' worth of midnight fantasies in which good girls did.

CHAPTER FOUR

RASPBERRIES. Normally raspberries did nothing for him, but on Lauren they tasted divine. Cameron angled his head and nudged her lips with his, surprised when they opened for him.

A wave of sensation crashed over him, more intense than he'd expected. Her lips were soft and smooth and sweet, the silken skin of her arms warm beneath his hands. Pulling her closer, he fully explored her mouth. He loosened his grip and felt her arms wrap around his neck as she kissed him back.

He hadn't thought ahead far enough to imagine what would happen if he kissed her, but it wasn't this. Hell, she'd been so annoyed when Anders had made his little announcement, Cameron had thought he might get slapped. He'd never considered she'd actually encourage him, match him move for move.

Sure, it had been a while since he'd had time to indulge in the fairer sex, but if he didn't know better he could swear she was sending him a message. Communicating with a kiss where words would surely fail.

What a brilliant way to communicate. This way he could tell her all the things he'd never admit aloud, even to himself.

The kiss intoxicated his already fuzzy mind, then made its way south at record speed, a destination too long ignored.

Their bodies fused together in an amazing stop-the-earth-from-rotating kind of way. It had been so long since he'd even considered being with someone, and now every healthy, young, virile drop of testosterone in him begged for a chance to play. His conscience stayed silent, as quiet as the world outside.

Excited by the possibility, he stepped forward, pushing her backwards until she crashed against the refrigerator. With a gasp that stole the breath from his lungs, she pushed him away, ducking under his arm and effectively putting herself out of his reach.

She covered her mouth with her hand, staring at him with eyes filled with emotions he didn't recognize. A look that rocked him to the core. Had he read her completely wrong, or all too right?

"Lauren, I—"

She held up a hand to stop him, though he had no idea what he should say. Apologize? God help him, he wasn't the least bit sorry.

With a slight shake of her head, she turned on her heel and sprinted out of his house. Cameron closed his eyes and hung his heavy head until it pressed against the cool metal of the stainless steel refrigerator. Blood pulsed, his heartbeat throbbing in his ears at the same tempo as the ache in his groin.

The bell on the front door jingled, turning all the heads inside Come For Dinner. Nyla Hart sashayed into the storefront, her blonde bobbed hair swinging against her heart-shaped face, and everyone behind the partition turned back to their work.

"Lauren, I'm about to make your day." Nyla's sing-song voice lilted through the room.

Lauren glanced at the bouquet of roses on the round table where she held tastings as Nyla walked back towards her desk. Glad Nyla didn't comment on the flowers, she clutched her coffee-mug and took a long drink of the brew.

"Ten bucks says my answer is no." Flipping open her binder that should hold details of twice as many parties, she knew she'd have to say yes to whatever her wedding-planner friend suggested.

"The Nelson wedding." Nyla smiled like the cat that ate the cream. "Jeannie said you did a wonderful job on the engagement luncheon yesterday."

Lauren narrowed her eyes. "The other caterer quit, didn't they?"

"Now, Lauren. Sometimes people don't have the same vision." Nyla shrugged off her black leather coat as she sat in one of the high-backed chairs opposite Lauren's desk and tugged down the sleeves of her black turtleneck sweater.

"She hated the petits fours yesterday." Lauren crossed her arms across her chest. "Ranted nine different ways about my incompetence with royal icing."

"There aren't any petits fours on this menu."

"I hate weddings." Lauren picked an imaginary piece of lint off her brown trousers and toyed with the brown fringe of her sash tie belt.

"No, you don't."

"No, I really do. I don't want to cater a wedding."

"I do." Diego chimed in from the back. Nyla's pale face lit up as he rounded the partition, wiping his hands on his apron.

Lauren shook her head. "Mrs Nelson's caterer fired her, and now Nyla is trying to get us to sign on."

"Are we free?" He reached around her, flipping through the book. "December, right?"

"The fifteenth." Nyla nodded with a smile.

"We'll do it." Diego said.

"Wait a minute." Lauren took a deep breath to keep from raising her voice. She loved both Nyla and Diego, but damn if it didn't feel as if they were manipulating her into something. And she'd had enough manipulation from Cameron Price to last her for a good long while.

He'd tricked her into more of a fake relationship than she'd agreed to, kissed her breathless, and then not called. Not that he'd said he would. He probably thought sending two dozen roses this morning would wipe the slate clean. But she couldn't do a thing about him, so she focused on work.

"We haven't heard about the location, the menu, the timeline, negotiated a price. You can't just sign on without the facts."

"Lauren, you agreed I could have more responsibility." Diego crossed his hands across his chest and stared down at her.

When she'd talked him into working for her two years ago, he'd had family responsibilities that had made the hours he'd have to put in working for a restaurant impossible. But with his younger brother now at university, his options weren't so limited. And she needed him to stay on, take on a bigger role to grow the business the way she planned. It was just so darned hard letting go of the control.

"I'm not saying no. Especially if you're willing to run the job. There is more to it than making a great meal. You need to get the facts first."

"I've got it all right here," Nyla said, pulling a PDA out of her bag and looking pleased as punch. "Give me an estimate, and I'll make it work."

"Did you two plan this?" Lauren looked between the two, who stared blankly at her.

"Nyla, can we fax you an estimate once we've worked it up?" Diego said with a smile.

"Oh. Okay. No problem." Nyla stood, slipping into her jacket and pulling her purse onto her shoulder. "Here's the thing."

"I knew there was a thing!" Lauren smacked the top of her desk.

"It's not a big thing. And Diego is so creative, it won't even be an issue."

"Don't inflate his ego, just spill." Lauren leaned forward, preparing for the worst. Like an impossibly tight budget or bizarre food allergies.

"The menu needs to be low-carb and vegetarian."

"With a wedding cake?" Lauren shook her head.

"It's a low-carb tofu cheesecake covered in sugar-free chocolate ganache and decorated with flowers." Nyla's smug smile made Lauren laugh.

"How do you do your job and keep a straight face? And how in the world do they expect us to do a low-carb vegetarian dinner?"

"Vegetarian or vegan?" Diego asked.

"I'll find out." Nyla's mouth twisted and Lauren huffed out a breath. This wedding was a nightmare waiting to happen. Complete with the mother-of-the-bride from hell.

Diego nodded, making Lauren realize just how unprepared he really was. He wanted to have more of a role, but in order for that to happen she'd have to show him the ropes.

"Let's arrange a meeting with the bride and groom." Lauren looked through her planner for an appropriate date. "We'll learn their preferences and arrange a tasting from there. Maybe even recreate a special meal."

Nyla pursed her lips together, but didn't answer.

"What is it?"

"The groom's mother is handling the menu," Nyla answered through gritted teeth.

"I'm out." Lauren slammed the book closed. Nyla knew better than to ask her to get involved in a disaster. And a bride who'd checked out of her own wedding always signaled chaos.

"What? Why?" Diego put his hands on his hips, his dark brow furrowing.

"It's not what you think, Lauren. The groom's parents are avid low-carb dieters, so the bride thought it'd be easier if they handled the menu."

Lauren grabbed the edge of her chair to keep from running out of the room. She could not work with a mother of the groom on a power trip. People went crazy when it came to planning a wedding, so Lauren avoided the situation whenever possible.

The jingle of the bell on the front door sounded, and everyone looked up again, this time at the jolly woman carrying the enormous vase of long-stemmed red roses. Three dozen, if she had to guess. Lauren recognized the woman from the early morning flower delivery, before the rest of her team had arrived for work.

"These are for Lauren Brody, again," the woman said with a smile, setting them on the small desk. "Where do you want them?"

Lauren raised a hand, ignoring Nyla's perfectly arched

brow and Diego entirely. The woman set the vase on Lauren's desk and handed her an envelope.

"You're very lucky," the woman said with a wink and a smile.

Lauren smoothed the white envelope beneath her fingers, the room completely silent except for the jingle of the bell as the woman left. She tried to rein in her hopes, knowing if the roses were from whom she wanted them to be from she'd have to school her reaction.

"Oh, honey. These are gorgeous. What did you do to deserve these?" Nyla fingered a blossom. Lauren barely held in the urge to swat her hand away.

"Did you know him before Saturday night?" Diego stared down at her, making her twist in her seat.

"Know who?" Nyla's gaze stuttered between Lauren and Diego. "You didn't tell me you met someone."

"Are those from him too?" Ricky asked, leaning over the partition.

Lauren clutched the card in her hand. The first envelope held his business card, nothing more. She wanted to keep whatever this envelope held to herself in case it was some sort of business contract. But then, who sent a contract with roses? She blinked away the thought. A man who arranged fake relationships and then kissed you breathless, that was who.

"You're really serious about him, aren't you?" Diego shook his head, annoyance coating every feature.

"Hold the phone. Who's sending you roses?" Nyla's eyes widened so much Lauren thought they might burst out of her head. "Who is he?" Nyla rounded the desk. "Why haven't I met him?" She stuck out her full bottom lip.

"Because he's either some big secret she's been keeping for a while, or aliens have invaded her body." Diego shifted his weight from one foot to the other. "What's really going on with you and Price?"

Lauren decided the envelope was the easiest route at this juncture. After all, if he'd changed the plan she didn't have nearly as much explaining to do.

The computer-printed note let her down. She'd so wanted to see his handwriting. A romantic notion, she knew. But she wanted to think he'd done more than had his assistant make a call. It didn't matter what she wanted.

"Meet me for dinner, and a proposal."

The exclusive and pricey restaurant he listed made her smile. He wouldn't find a thing he'd be willing to eat on the menu. Everything required delicate attention. Unless he'd chosen it because he didn't want to pay her too much notice.

She didn't know quite what she'd gotten herself into with Cameron and this scheme, or if she'd be able to keep her attraction to him in check if he made a move on her again. But before she took the safe path and bowed out, she wanted to find out just what he had to say.

"Oh my God. You are serious about him!" Nyla wrapped her up in a hug that proved nearly impossible to shrug off. Finally, she stepped away, grabbing her PDA. "When are you thinking?"

"Thinking?" She wasn't thinking anything but that a cute guy had asked her to have a fun evening that had rapidly spiraled out of their control. If she'd been thinking, she would have thought of a better solution than being his fake girlfriend in the first place.

"For the perfect wedding."

"Uh-uh. No wedding." Fake girlfriend she could pull off if given proper incentive. But no fake weddings. There she drew the line.

"I don't need a perfect wedding. Or any wedding at all. I'm dating someone." Or not. "That doesn't always lead to the picket fence and mini-van."

"We should do it at your mom's house. In the garden in the spring. Can you wait until spring?"

Lauren sat up straight and prepared her best bossy voice. "Nyla, there will be no wedding."

"But it would mean so much to your mom."

"Don't make me feel guilty." Lauren hadn't thought about telling her mother about Cameron. But she had to now. Her mother might rarely leave the house, but she knew everything about the Seattle social grapevine.

"This could be so good for her." Nyla smiled. Lauren had to stop this train of thought.

"You're encouraging me to date Cameron, and yet you don't know him. You don't know what he does, how he treats me, who he is. You only care that I eventually get a ring on my finger so you can plan the party."

"You're overreacting. I trust your judgment with men. That's why I'm not pushing to meet him. And for the record, you're not volunteering any information either."

The door stole their attention as the bell announced another visitor. The same happy woman entered with an identical bouquet. She nudged Lauren's appointment book as she set down the vase and passed her another envelope.

"There's a phone number at the bottom, honey. You're supposed to call him." The woman winked and grinned, making her way out of the shop.

"Call him!" Nyla demanded.

"No." Lauren would call, but not with an audience. And not until she was good and ready.

"Why not? Are you having cold feet?"

"You have to at least call and thank him for the flowers." Ricky's head peeked out from the kitchen.

"Leave me alone, all of you." Lauren pushed each vase to opposite sides of her desk and opened her planner, trying to get some work done beneath the blooms. Nyla simply stared at her, no doubt forming her argument with each tap of her black suede boot against the floor.

Sliding the envelope beneath the planner, Lauren tried to focus on ordering enough plates and tables from the rental company for the parties they were catering next week. After filling out the forms she stood and walked to the fax machine.

On top of the machine sat the Come For Dinner lunch menu. Lauren fingered the flyer, a wicked plan forming in her mind. Cameron had agreed she'd get Anders & Norton business as well. Pulling his business card out of her pocket, Lauren scrawled a cover page saying little more than his name and hers. With a triumphant smile she dialed the number, listening to the electronic beep and groan as the machine did its job.

Looking out of the front windows, she froze as she spied the white delivery van out front, again. Seconds later in walked the same cheery woman and the same bouquet of red roses. She set the vase smack in the middle of Lauren's desk, then crossed the small room to hand her an envelope.

"I think he plans on keeping this up all day. Which is fine by me, but most women start to give in after the second delivery."

Lauren turned the envelope over in her hand. Inside was a note with one word. "Please." "Does he have you come every half-hour until he calls it off?"

"Not exactly. He calls with a new message each time."

Oh. So he was putting some effort into this. Well. That changed everything. Lauren crossed to her desk, flipping through her files for the addresses she needed.

She pulled out a sheet of stationery and quickly scribbled a message of her own. One that included the address of her favorite restaurant. If he wanted to see her, he'd need to make an effort.

"Let's try something a little different with the next delivery, shall we?"

CHAPTER FIVE

HAVING an affair with Cameron Price would break every dating rule Lauren had ever tried to live by. And yet as she bustled down the busy sidewalk towards the restaurant she couldn't get the idea out of her mind. Cameron fit the mold of what she wanted in a man in every way but one. He'd stated a relationship didn't interest him.

Maybe she was drawn to emotionally unavailable men. In between building her business, keeping up with her friends, logging time on the treadmill at the gym, keeping up on the latest bestseller, television craze, celebrity scandal and fad diet, she had little time to search out the perfect man.

The conservative, educated, successful men she'd dated all claimed to want an equal partner, until they realized just how many hours it took to run your own business. They expected her to understand about their busy schedules and demanding clients, but that understanding had never been reciprocated. Since opening Come For Dinner she hadn't been able to find someone willing to accept the time she had left when her workday ended.

But Cameron didn't want a full-time relationship.

Perhaps that created the urge propelling her naughty thoughts. At most, he wanted a part-time dalliance. And that was all Lauren had energy for. It could be the perfect solution to the confusing predicament they found themselves in.

It sounded simple in her head, but Lauren had no idea how to approach the topic with Cameron. They were attracted to each other. He'd proven that with the kiss that had had her running scared before she'd done something truly humiliating, such as strip him naked and take him on the kitchen floor. Tonight he'd want to get their stories straight about the break-up. How could she convince him to let the game play out a while longer?

Lauren found herself in front of the restaurant, with no time left to formulate a plan. Probably best not to get her hopes up and to play it by ear anyway. Catching her reflection in the glass, she ran a hand through the loose waves of her hair and straightened her coat. And then spied Cameron already inside.

As if he could feel the weight of her stare, Cameron turned in his seat. His gaze burned into hers, searing the moment in her memory. The smile on his lips went beyond charismatic. It showed his power, magnetism, ability to make her abandon everything she'd ever known to be right in favor of a chance to indulge her stifled wild side.

He rose from his seat and she quickly made her way inside the warm restaurant, walking directly to his table. The comforting scents of baking bread and fresh garlic protected her from his pheromones as she stood before him, drinking in the appreciative gleam in his eye as his gaze dripped over her body.

When she'd dressed this morning, the low-rise boot-cut

brown trousers and long-sleeved fitted brown sweater had been nothing but practical. A frame for the fun touches of the sash tied low on her hips, the pointy-toe high-heel brown leather boots, and the fantastic crochet-trimmed coat. Her love of clothes came in handy for the impromptu dinner date.

Cameron must have a similar appreciation for appearances. He looked magnificent in his olive wool trousers and French blue shirt, which brought out the striking blue of his eyes. The handkerchief in his suit-coat pocket matched his shirt perfectly, the patterned tie picking up both the olive of his suit and the blue of his shirt. The man could pose for a catalog.

Though she always went for conservative types, dress casual ruled the land. Shame more men didn't realize the appeal of a well-tailored suit. Cameron in such a package made her heart lurch and her pulse throb. With every second in his presence, indulging in an affair became a better and better idea.

Cameron stepped to the side, pulling out her chair from the small table. The expression on his chiseled face was tranquil, almost cold, but she knew heat simmered beneath the planes of muscle and full mouth. As collected as he pretended to be, he must be as tempted as she was to take this from fake to real.

"You're tall," he said with a half-smile.

Lauren blinked, realizing how much she'd read into his look. Ridiculous, hopeful notions. "I'm wearing heels."

After she sat, he pushed her chair in and took his own. Steepling his fingers, Cameron sat back in his chair and let out a long, slow breath. His stare set her nerves ablaze with such ease it was a miracle she didn't spontaneously combust.

Damn. She needed to get some perspective. He'd come for a business meeting; she was the one turning it into a date.

Grabbing her menu off the table, Lauren opened it to shield herself from his piercing stare. She needed to ask him what he wanted so she'd know what argument to make when convincing him to give their charade a chance. But first she needed to collect herself. The man affected her in a way no one ever had, making her wonder if the attraction she thought she saw in his gaze was just her fascination for him resonating back to her.

"I had a talk with Bob Anders today." Cameron cleared his throat, but Lauren pretended to study the menu. "Your abhorrence of prenuptial agreements surprised him. He thought your family would insist you'd be protected."

"Did he?" Lauren laid her menu aside and pursed her lips together. Talking about her mother wasn't on the menu for a business meeting.

"I think I covered well, but it was a bit of a surprise. I'm wondering how many more you have for me." His eyes crinkled at the corners as he smiled.

Now that had to be flirting. "I'm full of surprises."

"You certainly are. Thanks to the way you directed conversation at the party you know a lot about me, but I know next to nothing about you. You're a fantastic caterer, have a flair for decorating, and since you sent sunflowers to my office I guess you like them better than roses. Beyond that, I know nothing."

Lauren set her forearms on the table and leaned forward. "Did you like them?"

"The flowers?" He shook his head and laughed under his breath. "I don't like the way they got the whole office talking."

"I should have gone with the daffodils." Lauren gave an exaggerated shrug. "Next time."

"Oh, no. No next time." The waiter arrived with ice waters, halting Cameron's protest. Before he could get another word in Lauren ordered for them both and sent the waiter on his way. "Did you just order for me?"

"Don't get macho. Since you've gone through life with culinary blinders on, I decided I would do you another favor and give you an awe-inspiring trip into the flavor zone."

He didn't bother to hide his laugh. "About these favors you've been doing for me. I need to apologize for the way I repaid you on Saturday. I'd been drinking and my behavior was out of line."

Lauren reached for her water and took a sip. She wanted to tell him she'd been in line right behind him, but didn't know if what he'd felt for her had been alcohol induced.

"Being with me for a while could be very good for you."

Lauren choked on her water, sputtering into her napkin. "Excuse me?"

"I know I said it would only be for the night, and I intended to use your break-up suggestion today with Anders. But he started talking about needing to see me balance work and my personal life before he passed the reins to me. So, I'm hoping I can convince you to play along for a while longer."

"Play the fake girlfriend."

"Exactly. I'm prepared to do what it takes to show my appreciation."

"Are you?" Lauren's cheeks tightened in a smile as she thought of all the ways she'd love for him to appreciate her properly.

"Is it too warm in here for you?" Cameron's expression showed genuine concern. "You could take off your coat."

What Lauren guessed had been a faint blush tinting her cheeks turned into a full-on flush. She swallowed hard, cursing fair skin and her dirty mind in equal parts. Standing, she took off her coat and folded it over the back of the chair. When she turned around to take her seat she stopped, realizing Cameron was staring, at her.

"You should play poker. You really had me going." Lauren took her seat and finally began to relax. His interest wasn't a mere echo of hers. He wanted her, and for a split second she'd seen it in his gaze.

"What are you talking about?" Cameron shrugged out of his jacket and loosened his tie.

"You like me. I bet that's why you chose red roses."

"I chose red roses because you decorated with them. I assumed you liked them." His gaze hardened, as if the wall around him became visible for a second. She'd stepped too close, and he'd pulled up the drawbridge.

"I do. They're my favorite. But when a man has red roses delivered to a woman, it sends a message. Were you trying to put on a show, or tell me something?" She wanted those flowers, his efforts, this meeting to mean something.

"Men aren't that complicated, Lauren. I wanted you to come to dinner so we could work things out. Next time I'll send tulips so no one is confused."

"Tulips in November?" She tried to hide her grin. Off-season flowers were pricey. Those sunflowers had been darned expensive "That will cost you."

"I can afford it. What I can't afford is for things between you and I to get cloudy. If you're not up for this, I completely understand."

"What is it I need to be up for, exactly?"

"I have events scheduled most weeks this month and

next at the house, and there are other parties and meetings to attend at various locations. You'll be showcasing your business at every dinner you host for me, checking out your competition when we attend dinners together, and gaining valuable business contacts while you are socializing. You're guaranteed the Anders & Norton account for the duration of our agreement, however long it lasts."

"Gee, what's in it for you?" Lauren shook her head, growing more disappointed with every word he spoke. Even though he made a terrific argument for this as a smart business move for her, she wanted there to be more to him than business. But he didn't seem interested in sharing that part of himself with her anymore.

"You'll be helping me more than I can help you, I know. Since you have money, you don't need the business—"

"My mother has money; I don't." Lauren had borrowed the start-up capital from her mother, but paid it back. With interest.

"Is there a problem between you and your family?" Cameron quirked an eyebrow.

"Careful, Cameron. Asking personal questions might constitute a date, and you seem intent on having a meeting." Lauren reached for her water and took a sip, hoping the ice would chill the anger she had no right to feel. He'd warned her he didn't want more. She couldn't blame him for her expectations.

Cameron took a deep breath and let it out with precise slowness as he narrowed his gaze. "Lauren, I—"

"You kissed me, really well. And you spent all day sending me roses. Why?" Seeing the turmoil in his stare, she wondered if he even knew.

"I wanted to. On both counts."

Before Lauren could respond, the waiter arrived with a plate of bruschetta and a steaming platter of spinach artichoke dip surrounded by tortilla chips and wedges of colored peppers.

"Would you like a bottle of wine with dinner?" Lauren asked, watching Cameron wrinkle his nose at the offerings.

"Yes. Should we look at the list?"

Lauren shook her head and addressed the waiter. "A 2002 Oregon Pinot, whatever you think is best." With a nod and a smile the waiter retreated.

"How do we know he'll choose the best one?" Cameron muttered, adjusting the gold watch on his hair-dusted wrist that probably cost more than her car.

"Have a little faith in people. Besides, you can't go wrong with Pinot that year."

"Do you have to know about wines for the parties you cater?"

"A little. But it's not hard. Two weekends a year the local wineries open up for tastings. It's a perk I get to call working." Bolstered by his admission he'd kissed her because he'd wanted to, Lauren decided to be daring. "The next one is Thanksgiving weekend. You should come with me."

"I'll be in New York." He dropped his gaze to the food, pulling out a tortilla chip unscathed by the dip. No doubt so he wouldn't have to pay attention to what he ate. Well, not tonight.

"With your family? Do they condone your annoying eating habits?"

"I annoy you?"

"The restaurant you suggested is very French. You wouldn't have eaten a thing on the menu." Lauren scooped up a helping of the gooey dip in a pepper wedge and hummed her enjoyment as she ate the delectable morsel.

"I'm not sure I'll eat anything here either." He absently rubbed the back of his neck.

"Isn't it hard to be a picky eater at business meetings?"

Cameron shook his head. "I'm not picky. I just don't want to have to watch what I am doing."

"Isn't that tough? Limiting your choices like that?" Opting to try the bruschetta, Lauren was careful to keep the diced tomatoes and basil atop the toasted slice of bread as she took a heavenly bite.

"Better to have something you know you can stomach than something that might make you ill."

"Oh." Lauren nibbled at the inside of her lip. She hadn't considered he might have good reason to be so picky. "Do you have a sensitive stomach? Is that it?"

"No. It's just best to go with a sure thing than take a risk."

"But isn't that what you do? Take risks on new companies?" Lauren had an amazing urge to free him from his rigid confines, to show him how much he missed by only looking forward instead of taking in the scenery all around him.

Cameron thought for a moment. "My investments are never risky. I only back companies that I know will succeed."

"And do they?" She flashed her best smile.

"I'm proud of my record, yes." The speculative gleam in his eyes shot through her like adrenaline.

"And what about me? Am I a good investment or a boring necessity?" Lauren fished a chunk of artichoke out of the dip with her pepper wedge, shoving the dip in her mouth to keep her from going too far, as if she hadn't already.

"You're not boring." Cameron hunted for another tortilla chip. "I never invest in a company I don't know as much about as possible. That's one of the reasons at Anders & Norton we prefer to entertain at homes rather than restaurants. People are more relaxed in that environment, and you can mix people together to make sure the right questions get asked."

Cameron leaned forward, his gaze as animated as his voice. "Take Friday's party. I'm looking for a company developing technology about renewable fuels. This company uses used cooking oil to power diesel engines. A great concept, but before I can sign on I need to know as much as I can."

Cameron gripped his water glass, tracing the condensation with his thumb. "So at the dinner will be an attorney and her husband, who just happens to be a professor in the field. A former CEO of a major vehicle manufacturer, a marketing expert for environmental issues, two of the potential investors in the portfolio who have expressed interest in mentoring the company, and the entrepreneurs who've designed the project. Because everyone comes from different backgrounds, they'll ask different questions over the course of the evening and I'll get a more complete picture than I would in a grill session."

"Grill session?" Lauren set her third bruschetta on her appetizer plate. She always ate when she got nervous, but she needed to pace herself.

"Firing questions at them across a table. Kind of like this." Cameron's businesslike expression softened as a slow smile lifted his lips.

"Ah. So you have decided I am too risky for you to invest your time in?" Her heart beat hard against her ribs as she waited for his response.

"I don't have the whole picture of you or what you

want from me." The salacious insinuation in his rich baritone warmed her blood.

"I want you to try the dip." She didn't dare tell him what she really wanted.

"Come on." He scowled, looking annoyed, a little petulant even.

"No, really. It's fantastic. And loaded with garlic."

"It looks like it." His lip curled as he eyed the plate. "I'll pass."

"You can't."

"I just did."

"Then you won't be able to kiss me tonight. If we both eat garlic, that's fine. But if it's just me, well, I don't want to make that kind of impression. So, eat up."

Cameron had never been so tempted to eat something in his life. But he could use any help he could get to keep his hands and mouth off her, so he shook his head and set his jaw. This was a nice woman, one who probably thought if she flirted hard enough he'd change his mind about having a relationship. And he liked her well enough not to get her hopes up.

She met his stare and held it, her petulant expression surely mirroring his own. Fighting the urge to smile, Cameron studied her face. Lauren possessed a beauty few women held, an intrinsic quality that lit her from the inside out. Her clear, pale skin radiated health, her narrow, small-featured face utterly feminine. Her pink lips morphed into an impish grin and he knew he'd won this round.

"You're going to be so sorry." Her smile gleamed as the waiter arrived, pouring the wine and exchanging one set of inedible dishes for another.

The waiter stepped away and Cameron surveyed the

two platters on the table. A bowl of pasta tossed with a dark orange sauce that looked nothing like cheese and a plate of dark green spinach, topped with slices of browned garlic.

"Accounting will be calling you tomorrow to set up an account to cater our lunch meetings."

"Cameron, you don't have to use us for all your lunches." Lauren scooped the pasta onto her plate. "I sent you the flyer to be funny. You weren't calling, just passing notes like a fifth grader, so I stooped to your level."

"What were you trying to say? You'd rather have my business than gifts?"

"I was trying to offend you and get you to call me. Didn't work."

He shifted in his seat. "No, mission accomplished."

"Don't do that."

"What am I doing?"

"Making me feel guilty. I needed to set a precedent. I want you to talk to me, rather than showering me with roses. Send me roses because you're thinking of me, not as a bargaining chip."

"I didn't know what you might say after the way I acted." He studied her response to his admission, seeing only the attraction he'd misread that night. Maybe he hadn't misread her at all.

"You know—" Lauren held her fork in the air, a piece of pasta speared on it "—as I remember it, there were two people in that kitchen."

"And one of them ran away."

"We needed to talk, and if I would have stayed, there wouldn't have been any conversation going on. Besides, I don't do regrets, and I didn't know you well enough to be sure I wouldn't regret it later." She seemed to notice the pasta on her fork for the first time. "You need to eat something."

His stomach growled in agreement. "Have you considered my proposal? Continuing the arrangement until I'm more firmly established here?"

"That is your proposal, Cameron?" She set her fork down with an exaggerated groan. "Fine. I'll play along on two conditions. One, you at least try to eat better. And two, we play this out and see where it goes."

"Play what out?" His pulse thudded in his ears. Did he dare?

"This sizzle in the air, that kiss from the other night, the way I shiver when you look at me. You like me, I like you. We enjoy each other. Let's see where it goes."

Cameron swallowed hard. Finding his mouth had gone dry, he grabbed his wineglass and gulped half the mellow red.

Attraction had been an implicit factor between them since he'd first seen her. Silent, building itself up with every touch, glance, fact he learned about her. And now that his desire for her threatened to break through the walls he needed to keep his life safe, she was giving him an ultimatum.

He wanted nothing more than to do as she asked, play things out and see where they went. Looking into her gold-flecked green gaze, he didn't see a choice. His passions had been stirred, the game started. The only way to ever know for sure if he'd learned anything at all from his mistakes would be to try with someone as worthy as Lauren seemed to be.

"I'd need an exclusive agreement."

"Of course. Honestly, Cameron, I don't have much time for relationships either. It seems like the perfect solution for us both, combining work and play."

"I agree. But if you decide you want to be with someone else, I need you to tell me. I don't want to deal with someone else's jealousy." Scenes flashed through his mind, fast and furious. He liked Lauren, but not enough to go through that again. Ever since he'd walked in to find his fiancée and his roommate together, he kept relationships very casual so not to risk reliving that moment.

"Same goes for me. Since our relationship is public, it would be too embarrassing to know the people I work for are whispering about me."

"Okay, then." Cameron reached under his seat and pulled out the itinerary of the next month he'd mocked up. "Here's the dinners and parties I have to attend. I'd like for you to make as many of them as possible."

She took the folder, but didn't look at it. "Not so fast. You have to eat something, remember?"

"You can't be serious."

"Oh, but I am. Butternut squash penne with sage and pine nuts or sautéed spinach with garlic chips. Your choice."

Part challenge, part game. She thought he didn't like to eat. She had no idea he could eat everything on the table. With deliberate slowness he lifted the plate of spinach and slid some onto his plate. The earthy aroma made his mouth water. The first bite was perfect, rich spinach, deep roasted garlic, warm olive oil, and they'd brightened the dish with a hint of lemon. He finished the serving before he looked up.

With a shake of her head, Lauren opened the folder. Her eyes widened as she perused the long list of dinners, cocktail parties, benefits and holiday gatherings. Her tongue flicked out, wetting her lips as she flipped the pages. Cameron closed his eyes and stifled a groan.

He was so used to shutting his responses off completely, cracking the door to his libido seemed to open the floodgates to a torrent of wanting. The strange feelings made him want to run. Straight to a bedroom with a door that locked and soundproof walls. Ah, hell, he'd reverted back to a teenager after knowing her for just two days.

"How can you say yes to all these people, and I can't even get you to taste pasta?" Cameron opened his eyes to see her playful pout, an orange-coated pasta tube on the end of the fork she held out to him.

"I need to establish myself, get them to trust me, respect me. Learn who they are so I can discover how to get what I want from them." He winced, realizing how cold and calculating he sounded.

"But you want something from me, need to establish a trust. Try the damn penne."

He shook his head, trying not to laugh at her antics. She thought she was goading him into something. In two seconds he expected her to call him chicken.

"Do we need to resort to playground trade-offs?"

He quirked an eyebrow, wondering what she had in mind.

"You eat the penne, I'll try something you suggest."

Cameron cleared his throat, coughing at where his mind took that suggestion.

"Fine. We'll do that. *If* you give it a chance."

"You have no idea what I'm thinking."

"Call me hopeful." She smiled, offering him the fork again.

Refusing her would be grounds to have his man-card revoked. Grasping her slim wrist, he steered the bite into his mouth. Buttery and almost sweet, a bit nutty and quite cheesy. He swallowed the bite and, releasing Lauren, scooped more onto his plate. He felt only slightly guilty she hadn't realized he'd eat just about anything.

"*Now* you want to eat?"

"You were right. I do like it." And as much as he would love to take her up on her offer to fulfill her end of the bargain, he needed to be sure she knew what she was suggesting. In the beginning women always said they understood his commitment to work above all else, but as things progressed they expected that to change. It never did, and they took it personally. He knew better than to compromise a woman who had every right to want more than sex, laughs and nothing else.

With a sigh she returned to her meal, disappointment obvious on her face. Suspicion niggled at him.

"Why are you doing this?" Cameron sipped his wine as if the answer didn't matter, when, really, her response could change the way his world rotated.

"Playing along as your girlfriend or offering to sleep with you?"

Cameron barely managed to grab his napkin as he choked on his wine. Once he'd contained his sputtering he looked at her through his watering eyes. "You did that on purpose."

"Of course." The feline quality to her grin set his blood on simmer.

"I need to know why."

Lauren sipped her own wine before answering. "I agreed to play along because it sounded fun, and you are very handsome."

"And now?"

She pushed her half eaten dinner aside and leaned forward. "I'm getting lapped in the dating pool by my friends. Following the dating regulations has burned me.

Neither of us has the time nor desire to dance around the subject. You want me, I want you, and everyone thinks we're together anyway. Why not give it a shot?"

"Because you know I don't have the time to invest in a relationship." He'd been honest with her from the beginning. He needed to know, not just the truth, but what motivated her actions to be sure he could trust her. "If you won't settle for less than a committed partnered relationship before, why settle for a temporary intimate arrangement that would keep you from looking for what you want?"

"Because life is short, Cameron." Setting her wine on the table, she leaned back in her chair and crossed her arms across her chest, drumming her fingers against her upper arms. "Maybe I'm admitting I can't have the career I want and the relationship I want at the same time, so I'm hoping for a satisfying compromise. Besides, it makes your charade much more enjoyable for us both."

He wanted to ask who'd told her she couldn't have everything she desired, who'd made her think she had to give something up to succeed. But her body language read full stop. And thinking about her situation made him wonder if he hadn't made the same exchange.

CHAPTER SIX

"THIS is it," Lauren said as they neared her building. She looked over at the brick façade of the retail storefronts that sat as the foundation for the high-rise apartments. She took a deep breath, pulling the clean scent of his cologne into her lungs. "I told you it would have been faster for me to walk."

"This is a great place to live." Cameron pulled into a loading area along the curb. "You can be home in a five minute walk, and I'm stuck in a car for at least ninety minutes a day."

"But what a car." They chuckled together as Lauren took in the spotless interior of the Corvette. Not a napkin, coffee-cup, or personal effect of any kind in sight.

"There's a huge SUV that came with the house, but I can't justify the gas it guzzles." Cameron ran his hand through his dark hair, pushing it off his forehead.

Lauren turned in her seat to face him. "I'm glad you invest in things you believe in. It will make the fund an easier sell for you."

"Driving a sports car is hardly practicing what I preach, but it came with the house. If I end up staying here very long I'll find something more practical."

"Are we talking about the house, or the car?" A new house would mean he'd stick around. A new car and things between them had a short shelf life. After his temporary intimate relationship comment she wondered just how temporary he planned on keeping things between them.

"We're talking about how many events you'll be able to make it to this week."

He grinned and her mind began to swirl with all the possibility his lips held. Straight white teeth, full mouth. Oh, my.

"I know it isn't much notice, but invitations were waiting for me when I got here."

"Ah, yes, the holiday season starts early so everyone can throw the same party over and over." Lauren dropped her gaze to her lap, where the folder of dates and places sat beneath her dampening palms. She wanted him to come upstairs with her, wanted to see if what sizzled between them would explode or fizzle out. But her imagination lost the race with her guilt.

"It's a busy time for your business, so people will understand if you can't make it."

But would he understand? Or use it as an excuse to find someone else to audition for the role of his lovely girlfriend?

"We should leave by four o'clock on Wednesday for the dinner in Portland."

"I'm booked for a retirement dinner." She studied his face as he gave a curt nod, revealing nothing about how he felt.

"Think that excuse will work for me?" He reached out a hand, pushing her hair first behind one ear, and then the other.

All the air rushed out of her lungs. With a simple touch the man could reduce her to a breathless, quivering mass of need. She saw the night unfolding in her mind, his hands all over her body, followed by his mouth, and then his—

"What about the rest of the week?" His velvet voice stoked the fire as he twisted a lock of her hair around his finger.

"That's good." She struggled to hide the hitch in her breathing. She only knew how to be so bold, and she didn't have half his obvious restraint.

"I'm glad."

Lauren stared into his heavy-lidded eyes, meaning to tell him she hadn't been talking about the schedule, but the words wouldn't form. Her mouth had far better things it would rather be doing.

The tendril of her hair slipped off his finger as he moved his hand to the side of her face. She turned her cheek into his warm palm and closed her eyes as the pad of his thumb rubbed across her bottom lip.

"You have the most perfect lips. Soft, succulent pink. When you're thinking, you bite your bottom lip and it drives me crazy."

She trembled at the words, his heated breath spreading across her face. He must be moving closer, must be thinking of all the ways she wanted him to enjoy her mouth.

"When you lick your lips I want it to be me. Hell, even watching you eat turns me on."

The sound of his voice, scent of him in the warm air of the car threatened to overload her senses so she didn't dare open her eyes. Dazed by the chemistry flowing between them, Lauren leaned forward until her lips found his on instinct. Her hands drifted to his body of their own volition, one palming his wool-clad thigh, the other gripping his silk tie to keep him where she needed him.

In his kiss she tasted the wine from dinner, the deep chocolate from the dessert they'd shared, and a desire so electric it melted her inhibitions. Soft as a question at first, but her answer was obvious to them both. He captured her lips, nibbled, sucked with a passion she'd only read about.

In an instant she lost all sense of time or place, exchanging kisses that taunted and tempted, diving into a sea of longing that threatened to drown them both. But what a way to go.

Lauren's hand slid up his muscular thigh. In their inopportune position with the center console between them there wasn't much contact, but she could definitely learn more about him by pushing her fingers farther down...

Fantasies spun in her mind. She'd dreamed of him on occasion, but never in her wildest imagination had she considered living the dreams, until now. Her hand moved higher until her fingers brushed against the sizable proof she wasn't the only one affected by the kiss.

Through the confines of his trousers she pressed her palm against him, curling her fingers around his erection. She ran her hand up, and up, and, oh, my.

"Are you smiling?" Cameron pulled back just far enough to whisper.

"We should go upstairs." Pressing her thighs together to stem the ache, she released him and eased back into her seat.

"Because of..." Cameron looked down at his lap and then back to her.

"I wanted to go upstairs since I decided to let you drive me home instead of walking." She met his gaze and pulled her bottom lip between her teeth.

Cameron's groan made her shiver. "Where do I park?"

Testosterone-fueled need battled with adrenaline-charged fright as Cameron let Lauren lead him through the front door of her apartment building and straight to the elevator.

There were so many things she didn't know about him, and, as dangerous as it would be to admit his weaknesses to her, having her find out the ugly way would be worse. Once the elevator doors closed, Cameron framed her face in his hands and pressed his forehead against hers.

"If we do get involved, you have to understand I will never want it to be more than casual." Her eyes widened. He knew he was being frank, but bluntness now would save them theatrics later on. "I understand if you need to change your mind."

Her head shook ever so slightly. "Did I tell you I've dreamed about us?"

"Last night?" So had he.

Her head shook again. "Since the first time I saw you. I wanted your bright blue eyes to see *me*. Even though I only watched you at a party, I knew something more lurked beneath your cool surface." Her hands snuck beneath the lapels of his jacket. "There is this wall you live behind, like a cage for a tiger. I want your wild side to come out and play with mine. We'll keep each other's secrets."

She didn't know how close to the truth she came. Before he could tell her, the bell dinged and the doors parted. Taking his hand, she pulled him down the hallway.

Excitement sparkled in the golden flecks of her green eyes as she handed him the folder and dug in her purse for her keys. Finding the prize, she unlocked the door and pushed him inside.

"Sorry about the rush," she said, flipping on the light. "Nosy neighbors."

Cameron laughed, setting the folder on the small glass table by the door, and turned to take in her apartment. Breath froze in his chest. Minimalist and modern, her apartment resembled his back in New York so much he felt more at home here than he did at the house where he got his mail. She'd been so attuned to him from the very beginning, he should have guessed her tastes would mirror his own. And with every moment he spent in her presence, his attraction to her grew.

City lights twinkled from the floor-to-ceiling bay window. He could even hear the buzz of bustling city life faint in the background. She'd used color well, blending deep red curtains with burnt orange chairs, natural wood floors and splashes of bright green in the pillows and throws on the brown chaise. From the granite countertops of her small kitchen, to the glass pendant lighting, everything was contemporary, yet casual. Perfectly Lauren.

"You like?" she asked, standing behind as she pulled his coat from his shoulders. He shrugged it off and turned around to face her.

"I like you." He slid his fingers through her silken hair, tilting her head to the perfect angle.

"Good answer." She gripped his tie, pulling him closer, but that was the last bit of control he allowed her.

He took possession of her lips. Her gasp told him his kiss was harder, more demanding than she expected, but since she followed it up with a moan as he deftly slipped her coat from her shoulders and slid his hands beneath her sweater to touch her soft, smooth skin, he knew she didn't mind.

Wrapping her arms around his neck, she returned the kiss with a passion that made his mind thrum with possibilities. She'd allow him anything, offer her body for his pleasure, only asking satisfaction in return. And since he intended to explore her body fully, indulging every urge he'd stifled, that would be his pleasure.

Moving his hand against the center of her back, he pressed her against him and deftly unclasped her bra so when he slid his hands between them he could palm her breasts and feel nothing but her velvety skin and hardened nipples. His mouth watered as he learned the shape, texture, weight.

He slid his mouth over her lips, to her jaw, nibbling at her neck, nipping at her earlobe. Everywhere he went she rewarded him with soft whimpers and breathy sighs. Her fingers pressed against his scalp as she held his head to her, her other hand struggling with the buttons on his shirt.

"Too many clothes." Her throaty whisper made him grin.

He released her and pulled back, locking their gazes as he undid the knot in his tie. She pulled at the end, removing it in a whoosh as he set to work on the buttons of his shirt. With a naughty gleam in her eye she wrapped the ends of the tie in each hand and pulled it taut. The corner of her bottom lip disappeared between her teeth.

Cameron shook his head. "No way. I'm using my hands tonight."

"I was thinking for me. I don't know how much more foreplay I can take before I knock you to the ground and have my way with you." She stepped closer, placing the tie in his hands. "This way I'd have to take it. Make me wait, Cameron."

He grew impossibly harder as his lips found hers again, giving her the only answer she could possibly need.

An insistent knock at the door made them both jump. Who remembered other people existed in the world?

"I'm not getting that." Lauren's hands went to work on the remaining buttons of his shirt. The knock became louder. "They'll give up, I swear."

"How do you know?" The rhythmic pounding grew more insistent.

Her hands stilled and she hung her head, leaning her forehead against his shoulder. "I don't know if they'll stop, but I really, really want them to."

Her wants went unheeded by whoever beat on the door. Reality began to seep through the hormones, making Cameron wonder if he hadn't been saved by the bell—or the knock, as it were.

Lauren stomped her foot against the floor and uttered a string of curses he never would have suspected she knew. Twisting her arms behind her back, she fixed her bra and pouted as she looked at him. "You're not the hide-in-the-bedroom type, are you?"

"Afraid not." Cameron tried to smile as he buttoned his shirt and stuffed his tie into his pocket.

"Lauren, don't make me get my key!" The door barely muffled the insistent female voice.

"Who's that?" Cameron asked, tucking his shirt back into his pants and begging his erection to disappear. Knowing the odds of that miracle occurring weren't good, he stepped behind a chair and hoped for the best.

"*That* is a dead woman."

"Trying to break down your door?" The knocking continued, no signs of relenting.

"I'm going to kill her, simple as that."

"So you know who is knocking." Lauren nodded, her hands smoothing her disheveled hair. "How long will she do that?"

"I'm not sure. Until I open the door, I'm guessing." Lauren stomped to the door and opened it a crack. "Go away."

"You're not getting married to someone we've never met."

Lauren stumbled back as the door pushed open, two small women stepping into the room. The tiny blonde with the heart shaped face looked embarrassed, but the brunette leading the charge seemed anything but.

"I am not getting married." Lauren followed them into the room.

"You said she was." The brunette turned to the blonde.

"No, I said she was dating someone and they should have red roses at the reception." The blonde shrugged her shoulders and offered him a smile.

"Enough!" Lauren's jaw clenched and she stood between Cameron and her friends. "Christabel, Nyla, you need to go back across the hall and mind your own damned business."

"Not a chance." The brunette sidestepped Lauren, quickly crossing the room so she stood next to him. "Are you playing some kind of game with my friend?"

Cameron shook his head and drew in a slow breath. How best to escape this soap opera unscathed?

"Christa! That is enough." Lauren charged across the room, leaving the blonde, Nyla, wide-eyed in the entryway.

"We're definitely not engaged. But we met over a year ago. I've been living in New York, which is why I haven't met Lauren's friends. I'm Cameron, and you are?"

"Christabel Kenney." She turned her narrow gaze on Lauren. "Is he why you haven't dated in a year?"

Cameron fought to keep his composure. She came onto him so strong, with such confidence, he'd thought for sure she played this game often. What did it mean that she didn't, that he didn't, and yet here they were?

Lauren reached for Christabel's arm, puckering the blouse beneath her clenched hand. "Can we please discuss this later? You've met Cameron, and now you can go."

Christabel shook her head, and shrugged off Lauren's grasp. "I'm glad to hear you are just dating, but that means we should all get to know each other. Has your mother met him yet?"

"I left New York on the red-eye Friday night." Cameron grasped the back of the chair, squeezing the upholstery in his hands. "There hasn't been much time for a meet and greet."

"Just enough time to start hooking up with my hopelessly romantic friend."

"Since when did you become a gossip?" Lauren moved to stand beside him, crossing her arms over her chest.

"Since when did you start keeping secrets? You're the most honest person I know, or thought I knew, until Nyla came home with a story about dozens of red roses and planning your wedding."

Cameron laid a hand on Lauren's shoulder and gave it a gentle squeeze, the muscles tense beneath his fingers. She looked like a cat about to pounce. "Ladies, really, there is nothing to fight over. Lauren and I are just seeing where this goes now that we are on the same side of the country."

"So we have time to plan an engagement party?" Nyla asked, her expression hopeful as she stepped closer, joining the conversation.

"We're not rushing into anything." Cameron offered up his best smile.

"Except a relationship." Christa's stare laid heavy on them both.

Cameron had to laugh; it was the only way he knew to break the tension. It worked, forcing even Christa to smile.

"So, Cameron, tell me, what do you like best about my friend?" Christa opened her eyes wide enough so he could see they were blue, but gave him no more. As difficult as Christa was, Cameron appreciated Lauren inspired such loyalty in others.

"I like the way she talks." True, and safer than mentioning her wild eyes or amazing figure, or even his unexpected need for a girlfriend.

"Me, too." Christa smiled and dropped her aggressive stance.

"What do you mean, the way *I* talk?" Lauren's puzzled expression made him smile wider. "Your New Yorker accent comes out when you talk fast, you know. The Harvard polish wears right off when you're feeling festive. *I* don't have an accent."

"Feeling festive?"

"Drinking."

"Ah." He looked to her friends for empathy, and was rewarded by their shy smiles. "I have an early meeting, so I think I'll leave you ladies to talk this out."

Lauren caught his hand. "You don't have to go. They're leaving."

Nothing could keep him in that apartment, with a battle about to break out, and Lauren affecting him in ways he could not allow. "I'll see you later."

He squeezed her hands, then released them, grabbing his coat. He walked out the door without looking back, not stopping to breathe until safely inside the elevator when he trusted himself not to run back into her apartment and take her up on everything she had to offer.

"You two are officially the worst best friends in the history of time." Lauren stood in front of her door and glared at the two women feigning innocent expressions.

"I like him. He needs a little help with his hair, but I can fix that." Christabel grinned. Actually grinned.

"There is nothing wrong with his hair." He might keep his hair a tad too short for her liking, but she didn't want Christa to add him to her list of clients.

"Except he looks like a stockbroker."

"He's a venture capitalist. Not the spikes and highlights type, so hands off his head."

"I'll leave his head to you, babe." Christa leaned against the chair and crossed her bare ankles. She hadn't even put on shoes to make this stampede. "But, I do want to know exactly what is going on. How is it you can be so serious about someone I've never met?"

"It just happened."

"That you met him, or that you decided to be his blushing bride?"

No way could she admit to both, so she went for the lesser of the two evils. "We're not getting married anywhere but in Nyla's head."

"So *that's* why you don't have a ring." Nyla slid onto the crimson chaise. "I know a jewelry artist who could design something for you."

"Cameron will handle that when the time is right." Another line she'd have to draw. No fake weddings, and no fake engagement rings. Some things had to stay sacred.

"It seems so out of the blue."

Part of Lauren knew Christa's worry had merit, but the part that had had her hopes pinned on fun tonight didn't care to have her motivations analyzed. Especially when they were so transparent. She wanted a friend with benefits. She wanted to be a naughty girl, the kind Christa could be without thinking, but Lauren needed safety and stability to manage.

She liked him, probably too much to keep visions of coupledom from dancing in her head. But she knew what she'd signed on for. She just didn't know how to make him offer up his assets again.

"Listen, Christa, I have my emergency preparedness kit. I know he seems like a flash flood in my dating desert, but everything will work out. No worries."

"I don't want him pushing you into things."

She'd been the one pushing. Not that he hadn't matched her move for move, but she'd love for him to shove her in the right direction. This time she'd get what she needed without the mess. Maybe it wasn't all she wanted it to be, but it was all she could figure her way into having.

Lauren drew a deep breath, the scent of Cameron's cologne still in the air. "It's late, let's all get some rest and pretend you both didn't just ruin my night like a recess monitor blowing the whistle in the middle of a pick-up game."

"In the middle?" Nyla frowned. Finally some sympathy from someone.

"No," Lauren smiled, remembering the glint in his blue eyes. "Just second base."

Hot water sluiced across Lauren's body, rivulets coursing across her bare breasts, over her taut belly, down her long legs. With one last rinse to her hair, darkened to a warm red by the water, she shut off the shower and stepped out onto the mat. Reaching for a fluffy white towel, she wrapped it around her body, tucking the ends across her breasts. With another towel she wrapped her hair, twisting it on top of her head.

A bottle of lotion sat on the counter and she pumped a

creamy pink mound into her open palm. She propped one leg on the countertop and began working the lotion into her foot, ankle, and calf.

Placing her foot back on the ground, she reached for the lotion again. With a gasp she froze, fixated on the image in the foggy mirror. She turned slowly to face him, a smile spreading across her face.

He lifted her onto the countertop, reaching for the lotion himself. Warming the cool mixture in his hands, the warm smell of pear wafting to his nose.

He knelt before her, giving the same attention to her foot, ankle, calf that she had. Then he spread her knees slightly, catching the scent of her arousal in the heavy air. Pumping more lotion into his hand, he applied it first to one knee, and then the other. His fingertips on the back of her knees made her gasp, pulling her bottom lip between her teeth. He continued his ministrations until her legs relaxed more, opening her to him.

Scooting her forward on the counter, he applied lotion to the tops of her thighs, the outsides, lingering on her hips, the backs, and then the insides, inching closer and closer to the heat of her.

Pumping more lotion into his hand, he lifted one of her hands from the counter and began making long strokes from her wrists to her shoulder. She shook her head, but said nothing when he arched an eyebrow. She'd asked him to make her wait, and he intended to.

His palms glided across her smooth skin, working the lotion into her other arm until it was soft as silk. With more lotion he went to work on her shoulders, massaging out the tension until her head drooped against her chest.

With one finger, he lifted her chin. Fire flashed in her

green gaze as he pulled back the sides of the towel, letting it fall to the counter.

She straightened her posture, presenting herself to him. It was his turn to shake his head as he stepped between her legs, reaching around to work lotion into the muscles of her back. She leaned forward, pressing her breasts against his chest. Her peaked nipples rubbed against his. In the mirror his darker hands against her creamy skin made his mind thrum with possibility, need. He didn't know how much longer he could wait, let alone make her wait.

He rubbed the smooth planes of her muscles to calm himself, not nearing the curve of her bottom until he regained control. She wiggled beneath his hands, writhing and pressing, and wrapping her ankles around his back, locking him into place.

He looked into her eyes, ravenous with lust. The world had melted so only Lauren, wet and willing, existed. Predatory feelings consumed his every thought so that nothing mattered, but having her, now.

Stroking the silken skin of her arms, he lifted them up and draped them across his shoulders so he could have free access to her pert breasts. He took a deep breath to steady himself, his lungs filling with the steam from her shower, the pear from the lotion, and her arousal. He ran a hand across her toned stomach, running his palms up until he cupped the weight of both breasts. In front of his eyes her nipples tightened even more, ripening into tight raspberries.

He drew circles with his thumbs, making the circles tighter with each pass until her fingers dug into his shoulders. The unhurried, purposeful exploration pushed him over the edge. He dipped his head, laving one ripened peak with his tongue. She arched against him and he pulled the beaded tip into his mouth.

Her moans echoed through the small room, making his penis grow impossibly hard. But he'd waited so long, he didn't want to rush over anything. Learning, teasing, licking, and sucking until he couldn't wait any longer.

Releasing her breasts, he trailed one hand down her stomach and the other over her shoulder to her neck, threading his fingers in her still-damp hair and plundering her mouth with a kiss. His free hand dipped down, down into nothing.

"Cloudy with increasing rain as the day goes on; heaviest from Seattle north through mid-evening, then widespread rain throughout the Puget Sound area later tonight. Lows tonight in the upper thirties to low forties."

Cameron sat up straight in bed, blinking in the darkness. His fist came down hard on the alarm clock stating six-fifteen in bright red numbers. He pulled cool dry air into his lungs, searching for the steam and pears, and Lauren.

Of course none of it existed. And it would have to end where his knowledge of her body ended. He shook his head hard, trying to knock some sense into his brain.

Throwing back the comforter, he stumbled to the bathroom and flicked on the bright flourescent lights. Setting the dial for cold, he looked down at his penis, straining hopefully against his belly. He'd been hoping only it was fascinated with Lauren; physical attraction could be ignored. Resisting her would be easy, if he didn't have to see her, smell her, wrap his arm around her at every opportunity. But dreaming about her, wishing to live the dream, meant an emotional, mental connection he could not risk. Ever. But did he still have a choice?

CHAPTER SEVEN

POTTED chrysanthemums stood cheerful guard on either side of the front door, their defiant blossoms issuing bright pink bursts of hope into the drizzly afternoon. Lauren held her key in her hand and wondered about knocking. Politeness lost the battle, and she unlocked the door, stepping into the warm foyer.

"Mom? Where are you?" she called through the vast house. Looking from side to side, she caught the rooms frozen in time. Not a photograph had been moved since the accident, but life changed anyway. The house, once so busy and bustling, now served as a shrine to what once was, and a warning of what Lauren could never let herself become.

"I'm in the den," Emma Brody called back.

Of course she'd be in the den. That was where the big-screen television, always tuned to the shopping channels, sat across from the computer where she did her Internet shopping. Four steps from the kitchen, and just a doorway away from the spare bedroom her mother slept in. The woman who had once hosted lavish parties and chaired community organizations had shrunk her world to an area smaller than most apartments.

Lauren walked across the mahogany hardwood floors, past the formal dining room table perpetually set for guests Emma never invited, and through the kitchen to the den.

"Hello, baby, I was hoping you'd stop by," Emma said without looking away from the shopping channel. She wore the same purple tracksuit as the woman hosting the show.

"I need to rummage through your closet." Lauren leaned against the Spanish-tiled countertop and pulled off her black ankle boots. "Care to play dress up?"

"What are you looking for?" Emma reached for a pen on the side table and jotted down the number of the item on the screen.

"Cocktail dresses and an evening gown or two."

That got Emma's attention, her smiling face turning towards her daughter for the first time. "Why?"

"I'm dating a man I can't afford." Lauren smiled, thinking of all the events she'd need to dress up for. She liked to dress well, but her closet barely contained anything formal enough for the occasions. Especially since so many of the other women would be in the latest designs. Thankfully, she and her mother were similar builds, and vintage was all the rage.

Emma stood, shaking out her chin-length gray curls with one hand. "You mean Cameron Price? From what I hear he can definitely afford to keep you outfitted."

Lauren's heart thudded in her ears. She'd come to tell her mother about Cameron, but should have expected the gossips to break the news first. Her mother might never leave the house anymore, but she was still as connected to the gossip grapevine as ever.

"Mom, things with Cameron are complicated."

"Complicated as in you've become involved in a relationship with a man I've never even heard you mention, or complicated as in you don't want to be another hand in his pocket?"

"Both, actually." Lauren tucked her hair behind her ears and met her mother's grassy green stare with all the indignation of a disgruntled fifteen-year-old.

"Then let's fix both, shall we? Have a shopping spree on me, and bring him over for dinner so I can get a look at him."

Lauren shook her head. "Let's see what's in your dressing room first, and you should come to the next dinner party at his place." That wouldn't be as much pressure on Cameron, and would get her mother out of the house.

Emma's curls swung to the side as she tilted her head. "You'd rather wear my dresses than pick out new ones? Really, Lauren. You need to get over these issues you have with money."

Pressing her lips together, Lauren drew a long breath and forced a smile. She needed to know she could support herself completely, without the safety net of family money. It was the only way to ensure she wouldn't end up like her mother, hiding inside a house because her world had died with her husband and son. If Emma had had more of an identity than being Senator Liam Brody's wife, she might have continued to live her life, instead of keeping everything on pause.

"Mom, I don't want to fight. I just want to look at some dresses, that's all. I'm planning on going to some resale shops, but you have such classic taste, and we're the same size, so I though this would be easier."

Emma nodded and muted the television. "You can have whatever you need. It's not like I'll ever wear any of them again. In fact, while we're looking for dresses for you, I'll pull out some to donate as well."

Lauren blinked, watching her mother walk through the room and up the staircase. In the last five years Lauren had pushed to donate her brother's and father's things. Maybe this was a baby step towards letting go.

Catching up to her mother, she followed her through the master suite and into the dressing room larger than the den her mother spent her life in now.

"Did you bring a strapless bra?"

"Wearing it." Lauren grinned as she undressed, watching her mother unzip a garment-bag section and flip through the dresses on hangers. It had been too long since she'd seen her this animated.

"Tell me about Cameron." Emma handed her a turquoise silk dress with a chiffon overlay, and pulled the hangers from three other dresses before tossing them to the floor.

"He's a venture capitalist from New York." The dress slid over her body and she stepped in front of the full-length mirrors mounted on one wall. Smoothing her hands against the gauzy fabric, she stared at the ethereal image. "This dress is a keeper."

"I thought so. Only got to wear it twice, though. A benefit in Seattle and the nineteen sevety-six inaugural ball." Emma handed her a black crepe mini-dress. "How long have you known him?"

"You know how I feel about black, Mom."

"Black isn't bad as long as it doesn't become a habit. Trust me, and try it on." She held out the dress. "How did you meet him?"

Try on the dress or confess everything to her mother? The dress won out. "This is so short it should be illegal."

"It's not that short." Emma adjusted the artisan pin at

the base of a deep vee neckline that held the dress together.
"Why don't you want to talk about Cameron?"

"Because it's not as serious as people think." Her mother's
eyebrows shot up. "His boss assumed, so now we're together
without any of the fun steps you take to get there." Lauren
unzipped the dress, quite proud she'd given her mother the
gist of the situation without anything specific.

"So that's why you hadn't told me?"

"I came to tell you today. I didn't want to explain over
the phone." She straightened up in time to watch her
mother dump a handful of dresses on the floor. "You really
are cleaning house."

"I think it's about time. And it's easier with you here."

She passed over a pink silk kimono dress. Lauren undid
the side closures and wrapped the dress around her body.
The cotton-candy pink of the dress made her hair seem
redder, her complexion healthier. Lauren scanned the pile
for more dresses and she held out an eye-catching lemon,
lime and mustard dress, admiring the wild geometric
design and banded collar.

"Baby, that dress is older than you."

"I don't care." Lauren hugged the dress to her. "You know,
Mom, you could sell these dresses and make a fortune."

With the first section of zippered canvas wardrobe bag
empty, Emma moved on to the next. "I'm giving you the
good dresses. Do you think Cameron will like something
so bright?"

"Probably not." She tried not to pout, thinking of his
ultra-conservative attire.

"What does he like you in?" She handed over a butter-
yellow wrap dress.

Lauren weighed her words as she changed. She needed

to tell her mother enough about Cameron to put her mind at ease, but not so much she'd need to backpedal if things blew up in her face.

"Cameron would never complain about what I wear. He's very polite, gentlemanly." To the point of walking out of her apartment after she'd invited him to ravish her. She shook her head to dislodge the self-defeating thought. "As long as I'm comfortable and confident in what I wear, he won't mind."

"Is his move to Seattle permanent? Or will you be traipsing back to New York with him?"

"I think he'll be here a while." Long enough to indulge her needs, and his. If only she could keep from panicking, or being interrupted by nosy so-called friends.

Emma smoothed the sash of the pale gossamer shantung. "Is it serious between you, Lauren?"

"Not yet, Mom. I promise, I'll keep you informed."

A smile split Emma's face. "I'm glad you're not rushing in. Take your time, Lauren. Be sure." She turned, leafing through the dresses again.

"I will be, Mom. You should meet him."

"I'm always here." Emma pushed a dress into Lauren's hands and turned back to the rack.

"You should come to one of the dinners, Mom. I could use some advice on adding color to his house. Everything is white." Emma froze, as in those bad sitcoms where they froze the frame so the actor could talk to the camera. "You need to leave the house sometimes."

"I leave the house." Emma pulled out an orange dress Lauren was glad to see go in the discard pile.

"Mom, you only shop online, even for your groceries." Lauren shed the yellow wrap, changing into the two-piece sleeveless top and long straight skirt. Damn if this wasn't as perfect as the last. "When was the last time you went anywhere?"

"Lauren, really. I prefer to be at home. You don't understand."

"Explain it to me."

"I've always wanted to just be. To read, watch movies, study Shakespeare, learn French, relax. My whole life was one event after another, life in fast forward. I can't rewind, so I'm pausing for a bit."

"Five years?"

"I don't have anyone depending on me, Lauren. As much as I wish it weren't true, your father and brother are gone; you have a life of your own. It's time for me to be selfish and do what I want to do, when I want to do it." With a quick nod to her head, Emma turned back to the dresses and pulled out a pearl accented cream herringbone knit.

"I worry."

"Let me do the worrying. Now, tell me more about Cameron."

Tucking her hair behind her ears, Lauren tried on the dress while she thought of something appropriate to say.

"You don't want to tell me about him?" Four more dresses joined the mountain on the floor.

"I'm not sure where to start." Admiring the dress in the mirror, Lauren caught her mother's suspicious stare and decided to go for broke. "He's very handsome, has these bold blue eyes that sparkle, and rich chocolate brown hair. He's impossible to overlook and has an authoritative stance that makes him seem arrogant, which I think he likes. He has a mysterious aura thing going on."

"Is that why the dresses matter?"

"What do you mean?" Lauren ran a finger along the scoop neckline, turning so she could scope the low back.

"Do you feel unsure of how you look standing next to him? So you thought vintage couture would make you feel better?"

"Mother!" Her jaw dropped open, her mind swirling because the comment hit so close to home. At the dinner party the other women had looked askance at her. She'd told herself being barefoot had caused their haughty attitudes. But she knew they'd worn designer fashions, while she'd donned a three-year-old simple black dress.

Cameron might not have cared, but the part of Lauren she'd thought she'd cast aside, the part that wanted to make her man proud of her, needed the dresses. She didn't want to think of it like that, but there it was. Dangerous, but true.

To correct her mother's mistake of hitching her life to someone else's, Lauren had turned her life on its ear, jettisoning her plans to marry and repeat her parents' life. But she'd become so frenzied with work and success she felt depleted, with little time left for herself. Cameron's proposal had been so tempting because she'd tired of her pursuit of loneliness, needed something to jolt her back into life. Even if it was a life she knew she couldn't have without losing the life she needed to stay sane.

"Lauren, you always comfort yourself with clothes. Have since you used to play dress-up in this very room. Is that why you haven't told me you were serious about him? You don't think you measure up?"

"I measure up just fine, Mother." Deciding she had more than enough options to get her through the next few weeks, she slipped out of the dress and stepped into her low-rise jeans. Pulling on the tweed off-the-shoulder sweater and adjusting the suede drawstring tie around the neck so it appeared to barely be staying on, she tousled her hair and turned to face her mother. "I'm quite the catch, you know. Rich mother, successful business, and no one has gone blind from looking at me lately."

"Lauren, really." Emma rolled her eyes.

"You deserved that." She stuck out her tongue and fluffed her hair again.

"What kind of events are these dresses for?"

"Dinner parties mainly. The odd holiday gathering and charity event." She'd reworked her schedule, having Diego run more dinners than made her comfortable, to attend most of the gatherings.

He'd been excited by the opportunity, and, with the crew in place and the menus planned, Lauren knew he could handle the responsibility with ease. She reminded herself she needed him to handle catering if she wanted to grow the business.

She wanted to jump on the make-it-yourself dinner cottage industry, but she hadn't been able to bring herself to let go of the catering side. That was, until Cameron had tempted her to step back and play with him.

"Are you catering these dinner parties?"

"All the ones at his place, and two of the others we're invited to. But Diego has been hankering for more responsibility, so he'll be stepping up."

"I'm glad. You work too hard."

"It will still be hard. Come For Dinner is booked for Cameron's parties, so I'll be handling them on my own." Which didn't intimidate her in the least. It would lead to a more intimate feel, and make their relationship appear closer.

"Do you have one this week?" Emma began packing the discarded dresses into one of the wardrobe bags.

"Yes, on Friday. He hosts dinners to get together potential clients and investors. This week is renewable fuels. Professor Volk is on the guest list." She smiled, imagining the face of her father's golfing buddy.

"Tell him hello for me. And make sure you prepare a vegan option for him."

"Vegan?" She'd been racking her brain for low-carb vegan options for the wedding from hell, running smack into a brick wall.

"He and Malta both. Actually, I'd guess a lot of people interested in renewable fuels would eat healthy, more sustainable."

No doubt, but what could she make that Cameron would be willing to consume?

"So, Mom, what do you serve a vegan for dinner?"

"You haven't looked up in four minutes."

Cameron blinked at his computer screen and cast a glance towards his office door. Lauren leaned against the doorframe, a vision in jeans, lace-trimmed top, and an apple-green suede blazer, a white box in her hands. He hadn't heard from her in three days, and she came to his office bearing gifts. He sucked his cheek between his teeth, wondering how to deal with the first meeting after coitus interruptus.

"I would have waited for you to pause, but I'm bored. This is the biggest, barest office I've ever seen." She scrunched her perfect nose. "Didn't you bring any pictures with you? A diploma or two? Something."

"I'll grab some things for the walls when I'm in New York next weekend."

"How was Portland?" She stepped into the office,

closing the door behind her. Walking to his desk, she set the box in front of him and perched on the corner.

"I didn't go." He turned to his computer, saving his work so he could focus on the conversation he'd planned to have with her tonight at the benefit concert. Talking without the chance of being overheard by the largest investors in Anders & Norton's projects held much more appeal.

Every moment since he'd seen her last, Lauren's proposition had niggled at his conscience. He had to be sure she wouldn't change the rules of the game after they started playing.

"You know I'm not in the market for a relationship."

Lauren quirked an eyebrow. "Good thing, because I could never be with anyone who throws business my way out of guilt. Really, Cameron, the caterer who usually handles the lunch meetings will be upset."

He furrowed his brow. "I promised you all Anders & Norton catering business, and I keep my promises." Cameron reached for the white cardboard box and undid the flap. Pulling the contents from the box, he found a turkey sandwich on whole wheat, a creamy potato salad with peas, and two brownies. "And the other service puts mustard on turkey. Quite the abomination."

"I'd have to agree." She grinned and leaned a hand on the desk. "You should make a list of your favourite food so I can plan menus and get your lunch order right."

"I'm not a picky eater."

"You have to be joking."

"I'm not. It's not that I don't like certain foods, it's just not practical to eat some foods during a meeting."

She sighed. "You could pay attention to what you eat. Actually taste the food."

He cleared off a section of his desk and spread out his meal. Making his lunch seemed very long-term, committed, intimate even. "Do you always make lunch deliveries?"

"Every day. And since you've contracted us to cater all lunch meetings, I'll be here every day." She tilted her head to the side, her reddish-blonde hair cascading over her shoulder. "I have a buffet set up in two of the conference rooms, so I have an hour or so to kill until I tear down. I thought it might look suspicious if I didn't stop in to see you, so I brought you a box lunch."

"You didn't do box lunches for everyone?"

She shook her head. "Enchiladas in one room, apricot chicken in the other. Pasta, green, and fruit salads. And brownies."

Cameron held up the tub of potato salad. "Did you make this just for me?"

She shook her head again. "We're catering seven lunches today, Cameron. We make huge batches, and then divide everything up. I opted for that because I wasn't sure of your stance on fruit."

"I like all fruits. But thanks for this anyway. And for stopping by. We need to talk."

"You want to talk more than any man I know."

"We're in an unusual situation, hence my need to clarify." He turned in his chair to face her, leaning back and steepling his fingers. "There are definite benefits to the arrangement for me. Having you in my life will make it run more smoothly, and pleasurably. But I still don't see what's in it for you."

"You don't? You outlined an impressive list of reasons over dinner."

Her cheeks pinked and green eyes sparkled as she rounded the corner of the desk and sank down in his lap with a mischievous grin.

"I'm not going to hate you in the morning, or expect you to deliver a proposal on bended knee with a three carat diamond. I like the freedom of our arrangement." Her fingers played with his tie as she looked up at him.

"I won't be asking you to come home early, you won't be telling me to spend more time with you. We enjoy the events you have to host and attend, enjoy each other on occasion, and keep on that way until one of us tires of the arrangement, or gets a better offer."

"No better offers while you're with me."

"Right back at you. What now?" Lauren pulled her bottom lip between her teeth and stared up at him.

"I think everyone buys our story."

"Including my mother, but I'm not talking about our selective storytelling. All of our little half-truths seem to have a way of morphing into extensive lies. The karma kickback on this charade will be huge if we don't start trying to make it true."

"That's what I meant about the way you talk. You phrase things differently than anyone I've ever met."

Lauren wrapped his tie around her hand, just as she had in her apartment. "What's the expiration date on your last relationship?"

"Expiration date?"

"How long were you together with your last girlfriend?"

He hadn't had a girlfriend in years, not since he'd learned, thanks to his beloved fiancée, that actually women saw him as a bank balance and not a person. Since then, he hadn't invested enough in a woman to care.

She wrinkled her nose. "You're a one-night-stand type, aren't you?"

Cameron ran a hand through his hair, pausing to rub the tension out of the back of his neck. What did he care that she obviously didn't approve of his behavior? The women never complained, never expected him to call. Women who needed the release as much as he did. Instead of answering her question, he snagged a brownie from his desk and took a big bite.

"I'm tired of playing solitaire." Lauren took the brownie from his hand and set it back on the desk.

"Oh, you mean—"

"Exactly. And since I have antiquated rules about sex hardwired into my DNA, I haven't been able to indulge. But what you and I have is a compromise."

"A compromise?"

"Cameron, you can't make fun of the way I talk, unless I can tease you about echoing everything I say."

His mind raced, disorderly thoughts racketing across his brain. He wanted her. Now. Often. But he couldn't risk getting involved, only to lose her when she traded up. He still didn't know what motivated her, so couldn't be sure the next man who came along wouldn't tempt her.

"What is it?" Lauren snuggled closer, the golden flecks in her green eyes gleaming. "I can feel that wall you build up. My lack of experience is a turn-off for you?"

Cameron shook his head. "I don't want you to be disappointed, to romanticize what happens with us. It's a business arrangement. I don't have the energy for emotional entanglements." She'd been so bare, so honest with him; he owed her at least the truth. "I don't have time to be that guy."

"I don't have time to be that girl." She smiled, moving

her hands to unbutton the cuff of his shirt and roll up his sleeve. "I have references. I'm a horrible girlfriend. I put in too many hours at work, take it home with me, can't be at your beck and call when you need arm candy. I'm fiercely independent, stubborn, and hate to have someone trying to keep tabs on me."

Cameron struggled to control his reaction as she moved to the other cuff.

"You can't be a good boyfriend; I can't be a good girlfriend. We'll save the dating community a lot of heartache if we take each other off the market. Besides, we *are* together."

He fisted his hands, barely able to hold back. "Lauren, I don't want you to make this situation any more complicated for you, to make it into more than you can handle."

"I know I can't cut casual encounters or partner exploration, but you and me I can enjoy." She went to work loosening his tie.

"Partner exploration?" He stilled her hands, wrapping his fingers around her wrists.

"You have to stop echoing what I say." Her voice trembled.

"What does that mean?"

She wrested her hands free. "That means I liked hearing you're not interested in being with other women while you're with me."

The surge of emotions heightening his awareness startled him. He knew this blinding rush of adrenaline, had lived through the torment it created, but couldn't understand why he felt it now.

Lauren stared at him and he knew she needed to leave, to get distance, both physical and emotional. He had to keep himself from asking all the questions he had, from learning too much.

"I didn't do it, if that's what you're thinking. My ex was cheating on me. I wasn't interested in being an entrée on his menu if it was à la carte."

The painful look in her eyes made it impossible for him to walk away. She'd been scraped as raw as he had, had watched her life implode. Cameron knew better than to find common ground, but damn if he didn't want to heal that hurt.

"Your turn." Lauren leaned her head against his shoulder.

"For what?" He tried to detach himself from the situation, to ignore the soft way she spoke, the warmth of her on his lap, wrapped around him as if she were molded to fit just so.

"Why did you say you can't get serious, can't see me with someone else?"

Cameron stared straight ahead, wondering how much to tell her. He didn't care to relive a single detail. He had to keep this from becoming personal. Professional and physical he could do, personal was not an option.

"You won't tell me?"

Cameron stared at the door, fighting with the part of himself dying for her to stay, wanting to trust her. He knew better. On both counts. "I can't."

"Okay." The look on her face showed him it was anything but okay. She reached for his hands, squeezing them in her own. "I need a key to the house."

"What?" That certainly screamed personal relationship, which they'd decided not to have, hadn't they?

"I could never be with a man who doesn't trust me with a key." Her grin lit up her face. "Don't you want to see what I'll do to the house before the dinner on Friday night?"

CHAPTER EIGHT

"Where is everyone?"

Lauren turned from the stove, watching Cameron saunter into the kitchen. His striped sport shirt must be an attempt to make the charcoal dress trousers work for casual Friday. Lauren grinned; Cameron's dressed down was dressed up for most Seattle professionals.

"The only car here is yours. And what is with all the poinsettias?" He leaned his hip against the counter, crossing his legs at the ankles.

"'Tis the season, Cam." Placing the lid on the pan, she brushed her hands against her apron and looked down at the white tank top and jeans she wore. Thirty minutes until the guests arrived, and she still had to change.

"I don't decorate for the holidays." His gaze cut around the room, and his nose wrinkled as he sniffed the air. "I'm confused. We have a dinner tonight, but no one is here and I only see one pan. It's a big pan, but still."

"Did you know you don't even have plates?" Lauren swung open an empty cupboard for effect. "I'm not suggesting we register for a china pattern, but serving guests on your own plates is a start."

He stepped closer, backing her against the counter. "You can have whatever you want in the kitchen."

A vision of taking exactly what they both wanted flashed through her mind, but they didn't have time to do it right. "Then I want plates, and an espresso machine."

Cameron laughed and shook his head, taking a step back. "You never answered me. Where is everyone?"

"At a retirement party. Dinner for one hundred. I took one for the team and opted to run this one myself. Unless you want me to switch with Diego. The guests are into alternative fuels, maybe they'll support your alternative lifestyle too."

"Very funny." His lip curled in disgust as she walked towards the fridge. "Can you handle the dinner all by yourself, and still be at the dinner?"

Lauren slid between him and the door to the fridge, crossing her arms beneath her breasts and lifting them slightly. His gaze dipped and she felt she'd regained some power. "I've got it all under control. I don't want you peeking and deciding what you will and won't eat beforehand. I want you to taste everything. That is my favor fee."

"And what favor am I repaying you for, Lauren?" The sound of her name on his lips made her want to shudder, but she suppressed it. She wanted him to see her as an equal, a partner, a friend, not some swooning woman he could discard like his usual one-night stands. She wanted him for the duration of the agreement.

Hell, she wanted him for longer than that. A shiver danced up her spine at the realization. She looked into his bright blue eyes and knew. She was falling in love with him already.

Preposterous. Unheeded. Definitely stupid. But that was

the truth. It made the way she'd been acting crystal clear, and yet complicated the situation in an entirely new way.

She'd been flirting with the potent attraction since the first time she'd laid eyes on him. Maybe her body had known all along and that was why the chemistry was so exhilarating. Her head knew things wouldn't work out well, but her heart tugged her in the direction of what it wanted. Cameron. An arrogant, inevitable, and completely unavailable man.

"Lauren? Are you feeling okay? You're white as a sheet." The concern in his voice and the warmth of his finger against her cheek pulled her from her muddled thoughts.

Her nerves jumped like water in hot oil, splattering everywhere. The same adrenaline response that had had her running out the door the first time he'd kissed her. She stepped around him, reaching for a towel, and began to wipe down the spotless countertop.

"I'm fine. I just remembered something I need to do, is all." Calming herself with a slow breath, she turned back to him and offered what she hoped to be a convincing smile. "Why don't you go upstairs and change?"

"What about you?" His gaze drizzled over her body, pausing at all the parts throbbing for him.

"I'll set out the appetizers. That way if anyone arrives while I'm upstairs changing, you'll have something to feed them."

"Upstairs?" Did his voice crack?

"I put my dress in one of the guest suites upstairs. Nice gym, by the way."

His brow furrowed. "Did you go through the rooms?"

"I haven't had time yet. In one room I saw your shoes so I moved on, the next gym equipment and a punching bag, but door number three had an empty closet." She studied his face, but realized he never showed any emotion he didn't intend for you to see. If she could get him to a poker tournament in Vegas, they'd both be rich. But then, he already had that going for him. "Relax, I don't snoop."

With a nod and a shrug, Cameron turned and marched out of the kitchen. Lauren's shoulders slumped as she exhaled and leaned against the counter.

She wanted to fall in love. Had always dreamed it would come on in a rush. But she'd also dreamed the man she fell for would be equally smitten with her. How naïve. Her heart had gone and jumped after a man who didn't have the time or inclination to catch it.

Running now would be the safest option. But running would mean never knowing what it was like to be with him. Even if he was pretending, she could live it for real. If this feeling only came around once in a lifetime, didn't she owe it the opportunity to grow?

He could never know her true feelings. He'd surely cut the game short in the name of sparing her. But she wouldn't be spared anything if she lost him sooner rather than later. And if they followed through with the plan, she'd be with him for as long as he wanted, in any way he wanted her to be.

Her heart flinched at the reality of her choice. She knew he wouldn't change; she wouldn't even want him to really. The importance of his career made him poor relationship material, while making him admirable in her eyes. She knew how hard building a reputation could be. It made her just as unsuitable a choice for him.

She saw no point in living in the past, or worrying too much about the future since no one was promised a tomorrow. What mattered was the present. And presently, she intended to pack a lifetime of memories into the short time she held the attention of the man she loved.

Lauren knew how to tease a man insane. Everything about her tonight seemed to be trying to seduce him, even the promise of getting whatever he wanted in return for tasting her food. Since the flow of air through the dining room felt like her caress on his skin, no doubt the salad, a strange concoction of weeds, seeds, avocado and oranges, was charged with the same sexual energy.

She couldn't expect him to eat and talk at the same time. He pushed the salad around with his fork, hoping to make it look as if he'd eaten as he tried to keep the conversation at the table flowing. But he felt the weight of her narrowed gaze, though he avoided it since he saw the challenge she set in front of him. Avoided her and the golden wrap dress she'd donned. It tied with a sash, making him wonder if he untied it, would the whole thing fall away?

To keep sane, he focused on work. Far easier to understand the motivations of the attorney, professor, former CEO, marketing expert and the entrepreneurs and potential investors trying to convince them all no better investment existed than using recycled restaurant grease to fuel automobiles.

"We're turning an environmental burden into a conservation benefit." Even in a suit, Henry Moss looked like a college senior who'd rolled out of bed and jumped into the only thing clean left.

"But this is currently a niche market. I can't power my car with cooking oil." He speared what looked like an orange and hoped Moss would delve into the sales pitch long enough for him to take a few bites. Avocado first. It would melt in his mouth.

"With the slightest adjustments, it can. Making those adjustments available to everyone is what we provide." Moss's partner, John Pratt, barely looked more presentable with his shaggy hair and fuzzy goatee.

"But what kind of traction can you show?" Dean Walters laid his fork across a clean plate and leaned back in his chair. The man acted as smug as befit a former CEO of the largest vehicle manufacturer in the country.

"For our size, we have generated significant revenue," Moss said, leaning forward. "Our profits will be exponential. The more people who take on the responsibility of alternative fuels, the higher the demand, and the easier they are to access."

"It's admirable, gentlemen." Professor Volk laid his napkin next to his empty plate. "We all wish consumers would be environmentally accountable for their choices. But Americans go for cheap and easy. The gas station on the corner is simply more convenient than the one alternative-fueling station in the metro area. There are many fuel alternatives—ethanol, natural gas, propane, hydrogen, fuel cell, electricity, methanol, and the list goes on. You have a double challenge, getting people to choose biodiesel, and choose your method."

To keep from answering the question himself, Cameron shoved an orange section into his mouth. Except it had to be the most acidic, bitter orange he'd ever tasted. Swallowing it down, he realized it wasn't an orange, but a grapefruit. Leave it to Lauren to find the one fruit he detested to make him look like a finicky eater.

Pratt cleared his throat. "What we are offering is ease and economy, a way to convert a consumer's existing car into a more efficient model. It's an investment that pays

them back in just over a year for the average person, sometimes as quickly as six months for commuters and sales
people who rack up the mileage."

Lauren stood, collecting the plates. Everyone else was
as enthralled by the debate as he should be, if he weren't
so distracted by Lauren. He had two options to get his
focus back at dinners. Either end the arrangement now, or
sleep with her to take the edge off. Really, he had no choice
at all.

"Don't do that!" Lauren struggled to catch her breath. Her
heart beat hard against the hand she'd pressed to her chest.
She stared at the floor, not willing to risk a heart attack by
staring at Cameron's luscious all-black ensemble.

"Help you with the plates?" Cameron quirked an
eyebrow and set the plates he carried on the counter. He had
no idea how much his presence unnerved her, nor could she
let him know how startling it was to think about someone
and turn around to find they were right next to you.

"I have everything under control. Go talk French-fry oil
with the rest of them." Lauren quickly donned an apron,
scraped the plates, and set them in the sink to soak. She didn't
want to get anything on her gossamer silk dress, so she kept
the apron on as she arranged the plates for the dessert service.

With a leering grin, he stepped closer. "I'm distracted."

"We're not doing anything here, now. It's one thing to
fool around at a dinner party for friends, quite another for
business colleagues."

"Then let's get dessert over with, because I can't think."

"That's because you're hungry." She tried to hide her
annoyance by unpacking dessert from the cloth bags on the
countertop. "I'll be done in two minutes."

"What is all that?" Cameron's lip curled and she knew he wouldn't be eating dessert either.

"This is me, trying to help you. Just like dinner." She pulled out a cutting board and grabbed a knife. Spinning around, she took a serving platter from the back counter and set it beside the cutting board.

"This looks scary. That thing has spikes."

Clutching the knife in her hand, Lauren turned to face him. His eyes widened and he stepped back. "Let me tell you something about how these dinners work, Cameron Price. It's my job to put people at ease, so they say what they feel, not what they think you want to hear. Tonight's meal was completely vegan, from the salad to the paella, to make your guests comfortable."

"I didn't know they were vegan."

"Of course you didn't. You just read their proposal and wanted to hear more."

"Not really. I've researched this. They're a solid investment, even if they present themselves too casually."

"They're casual because they are comfortable. With you. Because they recognize the accommodation you made, appreciate that attention to detail. Even though you had three bites of rice and a grapefruit wedge all evening. And then made a face, even though you claim to like all fruits."

She turned around, slicing limes into wedges and arranging them on the edge of the platter. He could blow her whole dessert plan if he made a face.

"Okay, so I don't like grapefruit." He held up his hands. "And I liked the paella, but I was too busy trying to frame the tree-huggers as the smart business en that they are. They have no sales skills, and that's a liability to their product."

Not sure how to respond, or even where her animosity

came from, Lauren focused on arranging one of every kind of fruit on a platter. The weight of his stare, and his patience as he stood next to her watching, calmed her ire.

Lifting the platter from the counter, she turned and handed it to him. "Take this to the table, please."

"What's this?" His nose wrinkled as he took in the platter of exotic fruits. All meant to prove a point, the point being discussed all night. "What do I say when they ask about this stuff? A green pinecone thing, a rotten lime, decomposing banana, half-dried plum, an orange spiky thing. You don't really expect us to eat this, do you?"

"I could never be with a man who wouldn't try something once." Picking up a peeler, Lauren went to work on preparing the fruit. Her fingers worked, peeling and chopping, slicing and scooping. She worked so fast she had to pay attention, couldn't let her mind wander to why she needed Cameron to try the fruit, to know he changed his mind once in a while.

On her tray she arranged tiny bowls, shot glasses, and chunks of pulp. With the fruits prepared for serving, she stripped off the apron and returned to the dining room. The guests who'd been so animated during dinner, stared silently at the platter in the center of the table.

"I see I have your attention." Lauren grinned and set her platter down. "I've been following along, listening to the main dilemma of bio-diesel. Which seems to be to get people to try it. The you-can't-have-just-one-potato-chip effect."

"What do potato chips have to do with kiwano and cherimoya?" Professor Volk asked, his eyes twinkling. Lauren's smile widened, relieved she had a cohort in this experiment.

"There are hundreds of fruits in the typical grocery

store, yet we usually grab apples, oranges, bananas, and the occasional pear, because they are easy. Sometimes, the rewards of looking beyond the surface, of having one amazing experience, can change our entire outlook."

"Like our engine converter." Henry Moss sat up straight for the first time all night.

"That depends on if everyone here is willing to keep an open mind." Lauren leaned forward, clutching the golf-ball-sized purple fruit in her hand and shaking it to hear the juice sloshing around inside. "This is a passion fruit. Who would like a little more passion in their lives?" Lifting a plate with shot glasses of passion-fruit juice from the tray, Lauren took one and passed it around the table.

Cameron swallowed hard before drinking his, but didn't make a face. Taking the small victory, she continued.

She explained about papaya, mango, and carambola or star fruit quickly, learning most everyone had at least seen them before.

"This is a cherimoya, or custard apple. You can slice them in half, scoop out the seeds, and eat them with a spoon." She passed the wedges around the table, intent on Cameron's reaction. He took one tiny bite, as he had done with everything else. Though his face registered nothing, his fork went back to his plate and he ate the whole piece.

Another night, saved by Lauren. Cameron shook his head and climbed the stairs to his bedroom, wishing she hadn't left with the rest of the guests. As they'd tried the exotic fruits they'd brainstormed ideas to introduce the product to consumers. With the backing of a former automobile CEO, the company would have the connection it needed to flourish. One investment down in his renewable energy fund.

Only about ten more to go. The thrill of creating a fund he knew would explode shot through him. His reputation would be legendary. The technology fund he'd helped create with Anders fared well in the chaotic economy because of risks he'd taken. Learning beside Anders had kept him on the cutting edge of venture-capital investing, kept his finger on the pulse of the economy. But this fund was his alone. A managing partner answered only to the investors, and then, just barely.

With a grin he stepped inside his bedroom and pulled his sweater over his head. His pants and socks joined it in the hamper. Stepping across the dark room, he sat on the bed and stared out the window.

The clear night sky twinkled with stars. Outside, maple trees danced in the slight breeze. A smile lifted his lips. His bedroom in New York looked at a concrete wall. The privacy of it had been a selling point. Seattle had a few perks. Huge house, fast car, landscaped yard, view of the mountains, and Lauren Brody.

He liked the way she talked, walked, thought. And she was willing to have a business engagement instead of an emotional entanglement. He'd never met anyone so attuned to his interests. In every way but food. She seemed to take it personally whenever he didn't eat something she made.

Thinking of food reminded him he'd barely had more than fruit all evening. He headed out of the bedroom and downstairs to the kitchen, wondering what he'd find in the fridge.

Halfway down the stairs he paused. The lights of the dining room shone through the alcove. He'd turned them off, but he hadn't set the alarm. His eyes widened, his breath grew shallow as he inched toward the room in silence.

Soft humming sped up his already racing heart. Lauren had come back. He ran a hand across his bare chest and glanced down at his black boxer briefs.

Step by step he inched closer to the room, wondering where she'd gone, why she'd returned. Standing to the side of the curved entry to the dining room, he realized how addicts felt. He knew she could destroy him, and everything he'd worked for. Reduce him to nothing and ruin his reputation. And yet with a promise of pleasure so great, he couldn't resist.

She'd changed from the golden dress and now wore tiny white shorts and a plum lace-trimmed tank. Every time he saw her she wore a different color, and intrigued him in a new way. He still couldn't get a handle on her motivations or her beguiling proposal to move from a business agreement to an intimate arrangement, but with every second in her presence he cared less about why and more about how to make it happen.

She arranged the poinsettias down the center of the table, alternating the red, white, splotchy pink and purple plants. Before tonight he'd thought they only came in red. She made him want to know all the secrets she knew. From exotic fruit to plants to how she affected him so.

He knew he needed to make a noise or clear his throat, do something to alert her to his presence so she wouldn't be startled. But he couldn't bring himself to break the moment, he simply wanted to look at her. Her casual clothes, tousled hair, and perfectly sculpted features. As if she belonged here.

"Are you going to stand there all night?" She glanced over her shoulder; a hint of amusement flitted in her gaze. Placing the last plant at the head of the table, she turned, the awareness simmering between them heated to a boil. The suggestion of sex hung in the air like an unspoken thought.

"I made you a sandwich."

Or not. Cameron blinked, doing away with his lustful thoughts as he saw more of the room than Lauren. At one end of the table sat a sandwich and a bottle of beer. His eyes widened as he stepped to his prize.

"We need to do a tasting so tonight doesn't happen again."

Cameron chewed quickly, washing the bite down with a swig of beer. "Tonight was great."

"You didn't eat a thing!" She squared her shoulders and put her hands on the curve of her hips, baring a thin strip of creamy skin below her navel.

He took another swallow of beer to help him focus on talking and not the skin beneath her clothes. "I ate pinecone."

"Cherimoya."

"Tastes like a creamy pear." It tasted as she smelled in his dream. "Good stuff."

"Cam, you said you liked all fruit." She twirled the hem of her tank top with her finger, exposing more smooth belly. "I served a dozen tonight you hated."

He held up a hand. "In my defense, no one likes grapefruit. And I tried everything else." He returned to his sandwich. After a week of her turkey sandwiches, he doubted he'd ever be satisfied by a deli again.

"I like grapefruit."

"You like everything," he mumbled around his sandwich.

"I had to do something. All the experts were trying to outdo the others."

"They were trying to show who had the biggest brain. Be glad they didn't bring their scales."

She began to giggle. Her laugh had an inherently sexual

quality. Even considering how forward she'd been, she maintained a fresh wholesomeness that captivated him.

He laughed with her, finishing his beer. "You made your point with the dessert. Thank you."

"You're welcome." Her soft breathy voice caressed his skin, though she kept the table between them.

"But I'll warn you, these dinners are always boring. I've pretty much made up my mind on what companies I'm investing in. These are mainly to make sure what they've presented on paper and in meetings works in the real world, hence the experts in the field and in business. And I can't take the time to eat much because I have to keep things moving." Cameron stood, taking his plate into the kitchen. When he returned, the dining room stood empty. "Lauren?"

"Down here," she called out. Cameron turned, looking down into the sunken room containing his refuge. She arranged more poinsettias atop the white grand piano, all red this time.

He rocked on his heels, unsure if he wanted to join his two indulgences. It had been years since he'd played for anyone. His apartment in New York had an old upright where he decompressed every day after work. Having such an amazing instrument at his disposal was his favorite thing about the house. The only reason why he hadn't opted for an apartment in the city.

"This is the most pretentious thing in the entire house. Every time I'm here, this room irritates me. It's wasted space to have an entire room dedicated to a piano everyone gets to stare at." She turned to face him, her bottom lip between her teeth. "Sorry. I know you didn't decorate. Every time I step in here I see a million better choices."

"I don't."

"If you want, I could mock up a few. This room irks me." She sighed, and turned around, pushing the plants to one end of the piano.

Cameron slid his hand against the wall, turning off the light, the room now dimly lit by the light filtering in from the dining room. Lauren turned at the action, a sinful smile spreading across her face.

Sliding onto the bench, he dared not look at her. Something came over him when he played, the walls he lived behind disappeared and everything went into the music. His fingers stretched over the keys, itching to release the tension of the night.

He stopped thinking and just played. The lively Dvorak piece chose him, the music singing through his fingers. Visualizing the song in his mind, he concentrated on the chord progressions and scales. The notes turned to colors behind his eyes until his muscles relaxed and he could feel the first time he'd played the piece. Alone at his grandmother's, trying to plunk through the sheet music to surprise her. He breathed deep, the smile taking over as he finished and looked up at Lauren.

CHAPTER NINE

HOT damn. Who would have guessed Mr Buttoned-Uptight had magic fingers? The way Cameron gazed up at her rocked Lauren to the core. Listening to him play was like watching him exorcise his demons. All of a sudden, without explanation, she wanted to expose all the secrets she kept hidden. Those piercing blue eyes bore into her soul and made him impossible to resist.

Already off balance by his ability to play as well as any concert pianist she'd ever heard, she only managed a weak smile as he stood and stalked his way to her. His fingers were so nimble on the keys, his entire soul captured by the moment, and all she could think about was whether he could play her as well as he had the piano.

"That turns you on?" His velvet voice rolled through her. He stepped closer, the heat of his body spiking her temperature.

Lauren bit her lip. "How can you know?"

One nimble fingertip circled her beaded nipple, straining against the cotton of her top. He took a deep breath and opened his mouth to speak, but she couldn't wait. She had to kiss him now, while magic still hung in the air. Pressing her body against his to quell the ache pulsing through her, she wrapped a hand around his neck and pulled his mouth to hers. No uncertainty about his reaction, nothing coy and flirty about her kiss. Just sizzling, carnal pleasure.

She tried to push faster, harder, making her desperation apparent, but he slowed every move, drawing each taste, press, lick out as long as possible. Giving in to the inevitable, she sampled and savored, unleashing the desire she'd suppressed.

The tenderness of his kiss made her want to believe in something more, but she squelched the hopeful thought, letting her inhibitions fall away and dance with the sexy shadows they cast on the walls.

A rampage of sensations crashed against her with each brush of his firm lips against hers. The crisp ends of his short hair tickled her fingertips as she pressed him closer. His clean-smelling cologne wafted through her, mixing with a musky maleness laced with need.

Two seconds before she knew she'd go crazy from frustration, his hands found the hem of her top and slipped underneath, scorching her with the fervor of his touch. She responded in kind, allowing herself to feel the power in the lean muscles beneath the smooth skin of his chest, arms, back.

His warm hands framed her face as he broke the kiss and pulled away, staring into her eyes. There couldn't be much he could see, with all the light coming from behind her. But she saw more in his bright blue gaze than she'd expected. Pupils so dilated and dark opened the window to his soul and she recognized the fear embedded there. He'd trusted and had it turned against him, just as she had. Intrinsic and unexplainable, the way she knew him without facts or dates.

She felt herself sinking as she stared, the only sound his labored breath, or was it hers? Adrenaline surged through her, arousal and awareness building, though he didn't touch her. His eyes, usually bright blue like the center of a flame, darkened and deepened like the middle of the sea, pulling her under his spell.

His head dipped, breaking the eye contact, but not the spell as his lips traced across her jaw, down her neck with such precise slowness she had to shudder. Her hands drifted to his tense shoulders, urging him closer as she ran her hands against his firm flesh.

The warm wetness of his mouth lingered against her neck, while his hands roamed her back, ribs, stomach. When he slipped his fingers beneath the elastic cotton waistband of her shorts, she braced herself for the whoosh of air as he pulled them over her hips. She expected him to do the same for himself, but instead his hands wrapped around her ribcage and lifted her off the floor.

"On the piano?" She giggled as he set her down. She leaned back slightly, getting used to the cool lacquer of the baby grand.

In response he parted her knees with his hands and stepped between them, running his palms up the inside of her thighs. Before he reached where she needed him to, he rounded her hips, crept up her ribcage, a light sweep along the side of her breast as he reached up and gently stroked her hair. He touched her so tenderly her heart swelled, because she knew that a part of him wanted to feel what she felt. He just didn't dare give more than he could afford to lose. She'd learned that was no way to live. She hoped he'd learn the lesson without all the loss she'd had to endure. He palmed her bare breasts, squeezing her aching flesh in his hands.

Hot and wet, her mouth connected with his. He huffed a breath and began to chuckle as he pulled away and opened his eyes. Light blue, as everyone got to see.

"For once, we disagree." His rich baritone vibrated through his hands still on her breasts, throbbing through her body.

"What?" She barely had time to gasp as he bent his head and lathed his tongue across the beaded tip of her breast.

A quick puff of air against her wet, sensitive skin made her gasp. He treated the other nipple to the same teasing flick of his tongue, followed by the cool gust of his breath. All of her nerve endings fired as quickly as a bolt of lightning.

His teasing enhanced the nagging throb between her legs, but she didn't stop, urging him forward again. In so much of her life Lauren took the lead, and for once she reveled in knowing all she had to do was follow.

He turned his head, scraping the stubble of his cheek against her sensitive nub and her moan rang through the room. She grabbed his hair, arching against him. But he wouldn't be swayed. What she wouldn't give for a mirror to watch as his fingers massaged and pinched, his mouth kissed and nipped.

Thinking of what it would be like to have that kind of attention played to her clitoris had her widening her legs as the space between them ached and contracted. Her heart hammered out a rhythm all of its own, faster and faster until her body felt like a live wire, every inch of her skin sensitized to his every move. Anticipation coiled inside, ready to break free at the slightest touch.

Except to get what she really wanted, she needed him to lose the shorts. She found it hard to concentrate on touching him with him working such magic on her body, but she rose above it enough to inch her hands across the firm muscles of his chest, down his rippled abdomen.

"Not yet," he growled, gripping her wrist and placing her hand back on the piano.

"But I want—"

"I want enough for both of us right now."

Lauren found it hard to pout and breathe at the same time as he pressed her breasts together, flicking his tongue against one tip and then the other.

"I want to know every inch of you." His words were hot puffs of air against her slick, sensitive skin. "Your body is flawless; I want to touch you everywhere."

She smiled at his words, thankful for the low lighting. Let him think she was perfect. She felt that way right now, as if she'd been molded for his hands to roam her every curve. The narcotic pleasure of his caresses left her dazed, in a dreamlike trance.

"I can't get enough of you," he rasped.

"Then take more."

And take he did, leaning her back further on top of the piano, continuing his attention to her breasts while his hand went to her damp core. He traced her with his fingertips, slow but firm, exploring her nuances. She purred as he tested the waters, pressing his thumb against her clitoris as his fingers continued to stroke.

Each time she neared the edge he varied his touch, changing the pressure and taking her to new levels of arousal. She moaned, digging her fingers into his shoulders. Her hands crept down his body again, this time slipping beneath his waistband and catching her prize. She purred involuntarily, imagining how full, how complete she'd feel when he was finally inside of her.

Pulling his hand from her, and her hand from him, Cameron shucked his shorts and kicked them in the direction of hers. As he stood bare before her she couldn't look away from the desire smoldering in his gaze to appreciate his manhood. When he looked at her like that her mind thrummed, her stomach fluttered and he shook her to the foundation of her soul.

Before she could examine that too closely he spread her legs farther, opening her to him. The air was cool against skin so wet and slick. But the chill vanished as he bent down, pulling one of her knees over his shoulder, and licked her.

She shuddered as he kissed, licked, nibbled, sucked, worked his magic. Slow and thorough, he warmed every inch until she thought she might explode. He laid his tongue flat against her clitoris, and stopped moving. Lauren panted and writhed, waiting, waiting. Before she screamed out in frustration he pointed his tongue and started moving his tongue back and forth, faster and harder.

The waves of orgasm started slow, building on one another as he threaded a finger inside and stroked her there in time with the rhythm of his tongue. With each pulse of the climax her pleasure intensified, as did her moans. He'd made love to her with the piano, and then with his mouth.

The realization sent her flying. She opened her legs wider, arching her pelvis against him and crying out. The sensations, both in her body and mind, gave her a climax more intense than she'd thought possible. It changed her deep inside, heating parts of her she'd thought long frozen.

As the waves began to wane she opened her eyes. Her arousal peaked again. The look in his eyes as he held himself over her made her heated skin flush, then he positioned himself between her legs.

"Cameron?" She arched an eyebrow at him, trying to think through the orgasmic bliss.

"Lauren." He stroked her clitoris with the head of his penis, and she wanted to throw caution to the wind. To hell with consequences.

"Condom?" She pulled her lip between her teeth, knowing she risked breaking the mood.

And she had. His face fell so fast she almost heard it plunk on the floor. He took a step back from her as if she'd slapped him. She watched all the doors she'd managed to pry open with him slam shut as his gaze iced over.

"It's okay." Lauren reached for his hand. He let her take it, but held it rigid. His chest heaved with each breath. "We'll just continue this upstairs." She slid off the piano, but leaned against it, waiting for the blood to return to her feet so she could stand without swooning.

"I don't have any."

"Any?" Her voice went positively operatic.

"You?"

"I don't have any either." She shook her head slowly, staring hopefully at his powerful erection, still eager for action.

He rubbed his hand over his face, then across the back of his neck. She stepped closer, wrapping her arms around him so she could feel his arousal against her belly.

"That got really out of hand. I'm sorry. I shouldn't have—"

She pressed a finger to his still-damp lips. "I should have told you before I wasn't on birth control. I'll go in next week and take care of it, but until then it's on you."

"Just like that?" He peeled her hands away and stepped back.

"Just like that." Lauren pursed her lips, turned on her heel and marched into the kitchen.

He heard sounds coming from the kitchen, but didn't even want to think about what she might be doing in there. Packing up to leave, no doubt. And all he wanted to do was ask her not to go. Stupid, because he needed to get a safe distance from her and the bewitching spell she put over him whenever he was in her presence.

Next week couldn't come soon enough. The trips to San Francisco and then back to New York would do a world of good at getting his mind back together. Keep him from making mistakes like the one he'd nearly made tonight.

In this day and age, who in their right mind even considered having sex without a condom? Condoms were a part of sex, and yet protection hadn't even entered his mind. No thought had, just the need to be inside Lauren. At least she'd been aware enough to stop him.

He wanted her more than he could stand, even though he knew it could all blow up in his face. It made no sense, and he hated when things made no sense. He either needed to walk away—not bloody likely—or figure out what she wanted from him so he could stay one step ahead of her.

She didn't want a baby, though he could have willingly walked into that trap. She wanted his business as a client, but he would have given her that without her ever touching him. Could she really just want sex? A fling packaged to look respectable?

If that were it, he had to be imagining all the things it seemed she felt for him. The tender touches and flirty looks were all an act. Maybe she stayed in character when no one was around to get him to play along.

The light in the kitchen shut off, catching his attention. The sound of footsteps on the stairs called him to follow, but he planted his feet. She'd put her clothes in one of the upstairs bedrooms, and he needed to give her some privacy. If he didn't, he'd be on her again in seconds.

"Cam?" Her voice rang through the house, confident and sure, though after the way he'd acted she couldn't be.

The least he could do was apologize. Walking through the room, he stepped on his shorts and looked down at his raging erection. It still hadn't let up.

"Come upstairs." Trilling laughter laced her voice.

He had to laugh, too. Walking up the stairs with an erection so hard he could barely move would be hilarious if it happened to anyone else. Might even be worth it if he had any hope of getting rid of it. The idea of bending down to grab his shorts was as daunting as climbing the stairs.

What had he gotten himself into? Swooping down, he grabbed the shorts and carefully stepped into them on his way to the stairs.

"Cam?"

"I'm coming." *Not likely.* God, he was a sad lot. He pressed his hand against his crotch as he climbed the steps, hoping to stem the blood flow.

He'd never been so out of control of his responses. Especially since the incident. The flash of memory deflated his arousal in no time.

Ever since he'd been careful, making every decision in a state of quiet panic. By the time he reached the landing he'd completely sobered, found his head enough to know he needed to apologize to Lauren, and get her out of the house before he did something stupid.

Too late.

Still naked, Lauren lounged against the pillows of his bed, the duvet pulled back in invitation. The only light came from the bedside lamp, which she'd muted by covering it with one of the red scarves from downstairs. The effect warmed the room, brought it from stark and cold to vibrant and alive. Or was that Lauren?

Somehow she undermined defenses that had withstood every woman he'd ever encountered. Actresses, models, heiresses, high-profile business types—none had gotten under his skin this way. She offered him no more than they did, no more than he dared return. A simple affair, where they both had their needs met and then went their separate ways without any grudges. Except he had a sinking feeling his needs would never be met so perfectly by anyone else.

He wanted nothing more than to lose himself in that gold-green gaze, but he couldn't risk it. Earlier he knew she'd seen through the cracks in his façade for a moment.

He couldn't look in her eyes, at her nakedness, or even her glistening wet lips. His body had already thickened with foolish hope. His gaze darted about the room, searching the uncluttered nothingness for something to say. Studying the steaming mug and small white bowl on the nightstand, he stepped closer. What looked like hot tea filled one, wet snow the other.

"You are an enigma, Cameron Price." Lauren twisted a red curl around her finger, the light making her hair glow like fire.

"As are you." He dipped his finger into the ice, the crystals smoother than they appeared. Putting his finger to his mouth, he licked the cold sweetness. "What is this?"

"Granita from the leftover fruits."

"They taste better this way." He lifted the spoon from the bowl.

"You don't want to do that."

"I don't?" He set it back in the bowl, and turned, catching the flashes of gold in her green eyes. "Didn't you bring it up here for me?"

"Yes, but not for you to eat." She reached out a hand to him and he took it, lacing his fingers in hers, staring at the union. Her nails were short and blunt, but her hands were soft and feminine. She pulled him closer to the bed. "I wanted to show you I could give as good as I get."

"You don't have to do anything, Lauren." He smiled wistfully, his eyes roving over her body, wanting nothing more than a repeat performance of what had happened downstairs.

"Are you afraid of me?" No taunt spiked her voice. An honest question that deserved an honest answer.

"I don't understand you. I don't know what you want from me."

Her eyes widened, innocence washing over her delicate features. "I'm afraid you're over-thinking me. I'm a simple girl, really. I want condoms. There isn't much I wouldn't do for a condom right now." Her smile flashed in the dim light. "I want ten more hours in a week so I can do everything I do now, only slower so I can enjoy it more. I want a chance to live my fantasies, with someone who can make them come true." She squeezed his hand and stood beside him.

He captured her lips in a kiss that gave him more of an answer than words ever could. She wanted what he wanted. Uncomplicated. Painless. Unrelenting.

Her hands flattened against his bare chest, pushing just heard enough to break the kiss. "Why did you put your shorts back on?"

"I thought you were leaving."

She shook her head, sliding her hands down his body, slipping her fingers beneath the elastic, and dragged his briefs down his legs. His pulse soared, pounding in his ears, making his erection swell with each beat of his heart. She slithered to the floor, caressing his calves as he stepped out of the shorts. Her hands trailed up his thighs, pressing on his hips to encourage him to sit on the bed. Pulling one of the pillows to the floor, she knelt on it and took a sip from the mug.

Spreading his thighs apart, she maneuvered between them. One hand reached up, curling around his neck and pulling him down into a scorching kiss. Her mouth had a delicate, almost apple taste. Hot and sweet and making him want to feel the sensation on other parts of his body.

She broke away, grinning as she scooped the granita into her mouth. A chilled kiss greeted him when she returned. The texture of her mouth felt different at different temperatures.

"This would be even better if you had an ice cream maker." She sank down, sitting on her heels, her knees pressed together as her hands traced the inside of his thighs.

"Are you putting in an order? Dishes, espresso machine, and an ice cream maker?" He'd buy her absolutely anything she wanted if she kept this up.

"And a Christmas tree with lots of lights." Her bright eyes locked onto his with a lustful, meaningful gaze.

"You can decorate however you want for the parties."

"The tree isn't for the parties. It's for a fantasy I read about once. I want to make love beneath the twinkling lights of a Christmas tree."

A bolt of sexual electricity coursed through him, making his penis throb against his thigh. The tender, erotic ache intensified as he watched her coquettish smile, breathed in the clean scent of her perfume and the unmistakable aroma of her arousal.

She moved her hand, pressing it against his pulsing manhood. A tremor of desire quaked through him and he twitched anxiously in her palm. His hand covered hers, giving it an encouraging squeeze. The erotic charm in her gaze made him weak with desire.

"Cameron—" her voice was a breath against his lips "—do you know what I want right now?"

He cleared the gravel from his throat. "I have a very good idea."

"I want to share a fantasy with you, something I read about and always wanted to try. Something you won't ever forget." She looked away, a blush creeping across her pale skin. "Because I'll never forget the piano."

Neither would he. But before he had a chance to say so she started sipping the tea, one hand still firmly on his penis. That she'd planned this out so carefully, thought ahead as to his pleasure, made him hunger for her more.

Fire blazed in her eyes as she leaned forward, wrapping her lips around his penis and pulling him into her hot mouth. The sensation, coupled with the lush feel of the ends of her long silky hair tickling his thighs, had him hissing, trying to hold back from the overload of sensation.

He gasped when she slid him out of her mouth, the air of the room cool against the skin she'd sensitized. He watched as she lifted a spoon of the granita to her lips, wishing he were there instead of the metal.

Holding him at the base, she danced her tongue over his hardness, tantalizing him with the shuddering coldness of her lips and the wet heat deeper in her mouth. Quick sucks at the tip chilled his flesh, only to be warmed as she took the length of him all the way down. All the while her hand worked intently, stroking him.

Eagerly he spread his legs to give her room to do everything she wanted, only to have her move away for another draw of tea. Her hot breath against his thighs made him gasp and grip the edge of the mattress in hopes of finding the edge of his control. Losing it so soon would give her a terrible impression of his stamina.

She fixed her luscious lips around the head, soft and shallow at first, her lips caressing and her tongue lapping at him as if she could do this all night. The thought made him groan, and did she just laugh? Whatever it was vibrated parts of him he couldn't restrain.

To take back some control he reached for her, palming her breasts and massaging the ripe flesh. Rubbing his thumbs across her nipples made her moan, and that moan pulsed through him until he nearly came. Would have if she hadn't pulled away for the damned granita.

"I like hot," he ground out, rolling her nipples between his fingers and staring into her eyes. He felt it again, that swirling feeling of the world narrowing to just her gaze.

Her tongue lingered on the silver spoon. With a wicked look she set it back in the bowl and pushed herself up on his thighs. "I—" her frosty tongue licked his lower lip "—like—" before he could pull her into a kiss her icy breath chilled his ear "—it—" he shuddered as her teeth nipped his lobe "—cold."

She trailed her freezing kisses further downward, over his abdomen, inching lower and lower to where he swelled larger than he'd ever seen. God, he really could explode from this. Finally she welcomed him into her mouth, warmed from kissing his body.

Heavy-lidded eyes stared up at him, pleasure evident in her gaze. The look on her face nearly did him in. Threading a hand through her silken hair, he rubbed his fingers against her scalp.

"You should come up here, so I can play too."

With him still inside her mouth, she shook her head, and then released him with a pop.

"I don't multitask my lovemaking." Finishing the last of the tea, she placed the cup on the bowl and pulled the towel it sat on from the nightstand. Laying the towel on his leg, she sank back down on the pillow and her scalding tongue licked his sensitive underside from root to tip.

"Tell me when you're ready." She licked him again. "I want to watch you come."

"Watch?" He could barely keep his eyes open.

"I've never seen it." Her tongue flicked along the ridge, making his body quake with pleasure.

"Never?" No way. She was much too good at this to play the innocent. "But—"

She shook her head, keeping her flattened tongue on the very tip of him. "Think later. Feel now."

Her tongue circled around the head of him, then her mouth dove down, enveloping him in her glorious heat. She suckled him with complete leisure. Her lips and tongue applied tender pressure to intensify his arousal, one hand gripping him at the base, the other finding a place that drove him to the brink. Her mouth produced a heated pressure that sharpened into an urgent, reverberating spasm. The smoldering inferno raced through his body, rocking him from the inside out.

His thighs trembled with the force of what was to come.

He moaned her name and arched his back, riding the wave of pleasure she'd delivered. Her hands stroked him with a frenzied, delirious passion as his climax crested and consumed his awareness.

The sound of her contented moans sent chills through his body. Opening a heavy eyelid, he peeked down, catching her with her hand between her legs, her chest flushed with the tell-tale sign of her own orgasm.

"You weren't supposed to see that." She pulled her lower lip between her teeth, a naughty expression dancing in her eyes. He pulled her into his lap and collapsed back on the bed with her on top of him.

"You are incredible," he praised, kissing her forehead. She snuggled close, their legs intertwining as his heart rate returned to normal. He memorized the exact smell of her hair, a tiny mole on her lower back, the curve of her hip.

"I need to go," she whispered without moving.

He tilted his head, lifting her chin so he could look into her eyes. With a finger he moved the hair away from her lips and placed a soft kiss there. "I could never be with a woman who could do that, and then expect I'd let her go. You're staying."

Her giggle made his penis stir. He rolled her to the middle of the bed, anchoring her bare body with his leg.

"Cam, you don't want me to. I have to be at work at five. We're catering two continental breakfasts at eight."

"I get up early. No problem there."

"Why do you get up early?"

"To work out before heading into the office. Hell, we could carpool." He smiled, and his stomach churned. He shouldn't feel this way, say these things. He should encourage her to go, keep a safe distance.

"I need my car for deliveries. I have lunches too." She yawned and settled into her pillow. "You should stay in town with me tomorrow."

"Why, are there condoms at your apartment?" He swallowed hard, trying to keep this relationship between the boundaries she'd set. Sex and public outings.

"Nope. I told you, that's your responsibility. Though if you forget I'll run across the hall and steal from Christa. Be warned."

"We'd have more privacy here."

"True. But tomorrow is the Symphony Gala, and Sunday is the brunch with green hoteliers." She yawned again, trailing the back of her hand against his arm.

"We could stay in."

Her eyes shot open. "We have to go."

"I can connect with the potential investors another time. I won't be able to think until I connect with you—" his hand slid lower, gripping her tight bottom "—completely."

"But I've always wanted to go to the Gala." Her bottom lip fixed into the perfect pout.

"You want to go?"

"Please? I've always read about it, and my folks used to go." Her eyes twinkled with animation. "The cocktail party before, and then the symphony, and the dinner after is supposed to be almost regal. I'm sure you'll meet more potential investors than you plan on. Everyone with too much money is there."

"But if I can't think—"

"We can get ready together. That's more efficient anyway, since the event is downtown." She scooted closer, nibbling kisses against his neck. "Please?"

He rolled her onto her back, pinning her arms

overhead. "We have to be up in three hours and we don't have any condoms."

She licked her lips. "It looks like you're up already."

CHAPTER TEN

DIZZY from the mental storm of a day that would not end, and a complete lack of sleep the night before, Cameron rolled his weary head from one shoulder to the other before knocking on Lauren's door. Two hours late. Thirty minutes before the cocktail party began.

Disappointment showed on her face as the door swung open. The teal dress she wore made her look ethereal and divine. A one-shouldered silk gown and matching sheer chiffon overlay hugged her every curve. Her thick strawberry blonde hair a tide of sensual curls that made him itch to thread his hand through the waves. The way she looked up at him expectantly showed her singular talent for making him feel at once like the most handsome, desirable man in the world, and a total fool.

"I'm sorry I'm late."

"Late is a half-hour. You missed the time of your life, I assure you." Her lips quirked in a smile and she reached beside the door, grabbing a coat and her bag.

Stepping out into the hall, she closed the door. He stepped behind her to help her with her coat, which unleashed the hypnotic scent of her perfume.

She barely spoke to him on the drive the few blocks to the concert hall, hardly acknowledged his presence once they'd entered the building. Instead of waiting with him at the coat check, she handed him her coat and pranced across the room, laying her hand on the arm of a man who looked as if he'd stuck his finger in a light socket. Obviously he'd come with his wife, whom Lauren greeted with a kiss on both cheeks, but Cameron still felt stirrings of jealousy.

Wariness seeped in as he stood in line, watching her work the room. A physical relationship he could only handle without emotional attachment. He couldn't watch someone he cared about searching for their next target, the next rung up the social ladder. Because no matter how much money he made, or how powerful he became, he was still a scholarship kid from midtown. He couldn't risk feeling more for Lauren than he already did.

To his surprise, she stood next to him when he returned from dropping off their coats. She threaded one hand in his, the other around the back of his neck, pulling his ear to her mouth to share a secret.

"There are two fast-food franchise owners here who recycle their oil into fuel. You should get one of them for the board of the company you're funding. And a state representative writing a bill on alternative energy—she's the one in the corner with the dark hair. I can introduce you to her because she interned for my father, and one of my clients does the taxes for the other two, so we have an in there."

Not exactly sweet nothings, but exactly what he needed. His hand firmly at the small of her back, he steered them from one conversation to the next, thankful for her connections and support. Before the lights flickered, showing the symphony was about to start, he'd collected a dozen business cards, and passed out twice as many of his own.

He stayed close to her through the crush of people as they made their way to their box seats, thankful an aisle separated them from the other couple sharing their box. No telling what she might say, or how it would be interpreted.

"I'm leaving in the morning," he whispered, studying her face for a response that didn't come.

"No brunch?" She stared straight ahead so he ran a finger down her smooth cheek. Still nothing.

"No, I have a meeting in LA." He should be there already, would be if she hadn't been so passionate about wanting to attend the gala tonight. "I'll be gone all next week. San Francisco, Dallas, and then New York."

"Thanksgiving with your family?"

Was Thanksgiving next week? His life didn't stop for holidays. The storm of noise began as the musicians tuned their instruments. He leaned back in his seat and closed his eyes, trying to pull the different tones from one another in his mind.

The heat of her hand seeped through the wool of his tuxedo pants. He opened his eyes to see her gorgeous face had thawed into a smile.

"We have a dinner next weekend. When will you be back?"

"Saturday afternoon. But I cancelled the dinner at the investment bankers that night so you're off duty."

With a nod she took his hand, kissed it, and settled it in her lap. A simple act, more intimate and affectionate than he'd ever experienced. It had him interpreting every movement of the symphony in terms of his relationship to Lauren. The ups, downs, inconsistencies, and sheer beauty.

The bold harmonic explorations of Beethoven launched the evening. He tried to keep his fingers from twitching at the notes he knew so well, but gave up. Lauren knew he played, and no one else could see. Beethoven referred to this, his fifth symphony, as fate knocking at the door. But what did fate have in store for him? Bliss or abject humiliation?

The grim first movement flowed into the swirls of hope of the second. The conductor varied the focused intensity of the movement, controlling the surges of power. The insistent rhythm marched on, quieting and coiling with tension until it exploded in an exhilarating shout. The third movement relived the build, the tension peaking until Cameron feared he might snap. When the explosion of sound echoed the beginning, showing the joy of returning to the familiar, Cameron took a deep breath.

Was fate trying to tell him that if he dared to try love again, there would be a happy ending after his explosion? Or just the inevitability of losing his heart to rejection again?

Voices clamored in Lauren's head, vying for attention she did not have to spare. She struggled to stay up with the conversation with the industrialist to her left and keep tabs on Cameron's discussion with the wind-power broker seated next to him.

Dessert slid in front of her at two in the morning, along with a welcomed shot of espresso. It took every ounce of breeding and decorum she possessed not to beg for three more. Cameron was lucky—the gusty windbag he sat next to requested more espresso and he piggybacked onto the order.

As her conversation partner opted to attack his chocolate baklava Lauren concentrated on Cameron's lack of enthusiasm for the night's Moroccan themed meal. She'd guessed he wouldn't enjoy the soupy lamb tangine, and even pardoned his lack of interest in the mediocre tabbouleh, but he could have at least tried the Marrakech chicken or the zucchini with almonds and feta.

She decided to sacrifice her baklava since he must be starving. But he didn't even have more than a nibble of that.

"It's chocolate, Cam. You like chocolate," she whispered under her breath.

"It's too flaky."

He'd never make sense. He wasn't a neat freak—orderly, yes—but to starve himself because of drips and crumbs? As the music director stood and addressed the crowd of well-dressed patrons a plan hatched in her clever mind.

After two dull speeches and three rounds of applause the room finally began to clear. To save time, Lauren offered to stand in the coat-check line while Cameron took a place waiting for the valet. The valet pulled up in the Corvette just as she stepped beside him with their coats. Splendid.

"You don't mind if I drive, do you, baby?"

The confusion on Cameron's face was priceless. She sashayed to the driver's side and slid in, adjusting the seat with as much grace as she could muster. She tossed her coat and purse in the backseat, noticing they landed on a garment bag.

"What time is your flight?" she asked once he climbed in and closed the door.

"Six-fifteen. Why are you driving?"

Lauren zipped into traffic and set about her mission.

"Tonight went well, don't you think? I had no idea cruise ships were interested in more environmentally friendly methods of power, but it makes total sense. I didn't like the hydroelectric lobbyist, though."

Well, really his wife, and the way she'd looked at Cameron as if he were an ice-cream cone about to melt. The woman's tongue had seemed glued to her upper lip through the whole conversation.

"I wished you hadn't invited them to dinner."

"I want to bounce him off the wind guy, see how they bring each other out." He shifted in his seat, turning to face her. "Where are we going?"

"Can I have the car while you're gone? I'll drop you off at the airport, and even pick you up. When do you get back?"

"Saturday at three. But you don't have to do me any more favors. You were great tonight. That's more than enough."

"Yes, but after the way you've treated me, I deserve a perk." She swallowed her fear, turning down the familiar one-way streets and feeling more in her element. "Like driving a Corvette for a week. It really is the least you can do."

"I'm sorry I was late. Work was crazy today. An investor filed bankruptcy, which threw three companies into jeopardy. I've been running all day."

"Did you buy condoms?"

"I have to be at the airport in an hour."

He hadn't thought of her at all. Not a good sign, since all through her hectic day she'd been able to think of nothing but Cameron and condoms.

She pulled along the curb and took the keys from the ignition. Grabbing her purse from the back, she climbed out of the car.

"What are we doing here?" Cameron stood in the street, his passenger door open as he rested his hands on the roof of the car.

"Feeding you." Lauren slid her key into the door of Come For Dinner and stepped inside, punching the alarm code that activated the lights.

Close on her heels, Cameron entered the building. Leaving him in the storefront, she marched to her kitchen and checked the charts on the wall for what went where with tomorrow's deliveries. Snagging a boxed lunch for now, and a boxed breakfast for him on the plane, she grabbed some bottled water and watched his baffled expression as she stacked the items in a handled green bag. She walked to him and handed him the bag.

"We'll do a tasting on Saturday night when you get back."

"A tasting?"

"You didn't eat a thing tonight. I don't want that to happen at one of my parties. I'll pick you up and we'll do the tasting at your house." She stepped towards the door, but he caught her arm, spinning her around.

"Why do you keep doing things for me? What is it you want?"

You. You loving me and not caring I can't be what you need. "To be the perfect girlfriend. It's not every day someone asks you to be their girlfriend, you know. Most men ask you out for dinner, and you become a girlfriend by default."

"I'm serious." The tense grip on her arm, the heady stare showed he was much more than serious.

"I've told you what I want." Wrangling out of his grasp she walked to the door and set the alarm. "I'm buying a Christmas tree while you're gone."

* * *

Lauren pulled beneath the glowing streetlight along the curb and cursed at her early morning bad luck. She usually parked in the lot around the corner, but since she had the Corvette she thought it would be better to have it at the curb where she could keep an eye on it.

And now Diego had his eye on it as he stood on the sidewalk. She didn't need any lip from him, or anyone else for that matter. With barely a wink of sleep in the last two days, she didn't have the stamina to play nice. Gripping the cappuccino from the cup holder, she climbed out of the car and activated the alarm.

His grin stretched from ear to ear as she rounded the car. "What did you do to earn a Corvette?"

"Very funny." Lauren stepped onto the sidewalk and buttoned her leather coat. She glanced inside the storefront, watching the crew bustle about the kitchen.

"I take it you're not making deliveries today?"

"No need. Besides, I still have to put the menu options together for the wedding from hell." She tried to step past him, but he blocked her way.

"We agreed to do that together."

Lauren stood tall in her French heeled boots. "I included the menu you mocked up as one option. Can we discuss this inside? It's cold."

"I'd rather we do this without an audience."

Her blood chilled in a way that had nothing to do with the temperature. "What's on your mind?"

"The card shop next door is going out of business."

Lauren waited, staring at Diego during the pregnant pause, trying to figure out why the stationery store next door's problems were hers.

"I talked to the leasing company already."

"You want to run a stationery store?"

He shook his head and rolled his eyes. "Not for me, for you. Come For Dinner catering was just part of our plan. You wanted to run a meal-assembly business in tandem."

Her eyes widened in shock. She'd always wanted to expand the business some day. Not today, when she was so exhausted from chasing Cameron she had no energy to get through the day, let alone chase a daydream.

"We can start remodeling after the holidays and launch in the spring."

"I don't know if I can." She'd paid her mother back for the loan to start the company, and made a tidy profit even when business was slow, but not enough to remodel a space and in effect start a new venture.

"We can." He pulled his shoulders back and tilted his head, his dark hair falling over his eyes. "I want to be a partner in Come For Dinner."

Never in her life had she been speechless. He wanted her business. Her soul tugged in opposite directions, one half wanting to hand him the keys and become the kind of woman Cameron needed, the other screaming, MINE!

"That was the plan all along, Lauren. I'd work for you until Javier went to college, save up to buy in, and then take over the catering side when you rolled out the meal-prep side."

"Yes, but your brother started college in September. I thought you'd buy in slowly. How can you afford to buy in, let alone get the capital to make the improvements for the expansion?"

"I can get a loan."

"No, no banks. I don't want anyone threatening to take my business because we have a few bad months." She tugged at the collar of her plum turtleneck ribbed sweater, hot and choked by cotton.

"We have never had a bad month. The location is perfect, Lauren; we can't pass it up."

"The timing is all wrong."

"Not really." He shrugged, while she still wanted to scream. How could he spring this on her when she hadn't slept and couldn't formulate a proper argument? "We'll be ready for the spring, when all the moms need help getting dinner on the table and kids to soccer practice. Once a week they Come To Dinner, pack up their meals for the week in an afternoon, and they're ready to go."

"I'll think about it, okay?"

Diego crossed his arms across his broad chest. "No, not okay. I don't want to work for you anymore, Lauren. I need to have ownership of something."

"Are you saying if I don't let you buy in, you'll quit?"

"I need more than being your chef. I can handle the catering side so you can focus on making the meal-assembly plans. I've proven that with the dinners I've run. And I'll handle the wedding. I said I would."

"This is a lot to take in before the sun comes up. I'll need to run the numbers on the expansion, see what I can arrange for funding."

"Not from your moneybags boyfriend. He's a shady character and I want our partnership agreement signed before you get serious."

"I don't think you need to get a lawyer already. And he's *not* shady." Lauren pushed past him and into the building, the warm air rushing at her chilled face.

She couldn't even rationalize why she was so upset. Since she'd talked Diego into signing on for her catering company, the plan had always been for him to work his way into partnership. Just not yet.

Lauren set her handbag and cup on her desk and went into the prep kitchen to make sure things were running smoothly. Satisfied Diego had all the breakfast deliveries handled, she retreated to her desk and buried herself beneath bills, schedules, and shopping lists. But the idea of living her dream flashed in her mind.

If things went well with Cameron, she'd need to enjoy him for a while and work less. If they went wrong, she'd need work to bury herself in. Really, this expansion could be playing relationship defense, a protective excuse to back off if he kept holding back. Even if things went well, and she had Cameron to herself for a while, this business venture would have more predictable hours than catering. She'd be available for even more of his functions.

Soon her busy work was finished and she surfed the Internet, gathering information on the fast-growing meal-assembly food trend. If she'd hopped on the idea two years ago when she'd thought of it, she could be franchised by now.

The concept was especially hot on the east coast, with families looking for healthy options as well as singles tired of take-out. Researching the competition, she compiled pricing and marketing plans, and drooled over menus. She was the queen of put-together cooking, but with Diego's gourmet touch Come For Dinner would really stand out.

Casseroles and comfort foods seemed to be the mainstay. Profitable, but boring. They could spice it up with international foods and salads, more breakfast options for weekend mornings, maybe even work in delivery for those who didn't want to compose the meals themselves.

But where to get the money? She'd have to ask her mother

again. Not wanting to take advantage, she opened a file on her computer and began drafting a formal business proposal, just as she had when she'd asked for backing the first time.

The world moved in a blur until a cup of coffee slid next to her hand. Lauren looked up, smiling at Diego.

"I like the way you think." He smiled, sipping from his own cup.

"You like that I handle the business side and you get to be creative with food." She shook her head and laughed, wrapping her hands around the warm cup and took a sip. Cappuccino. How she loved this man.

"We're a good team, Lauren. I want us to stay that way. I'm sorry about how I put things earlier, about Cameron. I don't know what's going on with you two. He shows up and all of a sudden you're together, he buys you a car—"

"It's his car. He's out of town, so I'm playing with it." She sipped too fast, the hot liquid burning her tongue. Setting it down on her desk, she stood and looked about the near-empty room. Catching sight of the clock on the wall, she noted their wedding-planning meeting began in ten minutes.

Diego nodded. "I want to set this menu. I need to show you that I can handle the catering side on my own."

"There's no need. We're a team, Diego. You make the food taste good, I make it look good. I handle the logistics, you deal with the operations. We complement each other perfectly. I don't want to draw a line down the middle with what is yours and what is mine. We'll both do what we're good at."

"So we're partners?" One dark eyebrow rose.

"If we can convince my mother to back us."

CHAPTER ELEVEN

HOME sweet home. Cameron dropped his bags to the floor of his New York apartment with a thud. His oasis of order wasn't half as welcoming as he'd hoped.

Business meetings, site visits, client lunches, and too many hours in airports and airplanes had left him exhausted. Opening the closet, he hung his coat on a hanger and turned to look about the room. Exactly as he'd left it. Nothing had changed, except for everything.

Dropping into the sage-green love seat, he sank into its lush depths and leaned back, kicking off his shoes and running his hands over his face. He'd barely slept in almost a week. He'd been working hard, but what made him restless were the damned Christmas trees everywhere he went.

Pulling his phone from his pocket, he flipped it open. Thankfully there were no messages from work since he'd hopped on the plane this afternoon in San Francisco. Most people must already be gone for Thanksgiving tomorrow. The call from his parents in Hawaii must have to do with the holiday, too.

He needed a day to catch up on work, and Thanksgiving provided the perfect escape from the rat race.

His stomach growled, reminding him he hadn't eaten since breakfast. Too busy to break for lunch so he wouldn't miss his flight, and nothing but pretzels on the plane. He stood up and stretched, wondering if he had anything left in his freezer.

The buzz of the intercom stopped him halfway to the kitchen. "Cam, are you home yet?"

He groaned aloud at the sound of his cousin's voice. Of course Jeremy would show up when he hadn't called back. He'd talked to his parents last night; they'd probably passed on the information on his flight schedule.

"Cam? If you're there, buzz me up."

Walking to the intercom, he jammed his thumb against the button in frustration. He needed to think, sleep, and catch up on reading proposals. In that order. Not get persuaded into a happy family holiday at his aunt's house tomorrow. Which must be Jeremy's mission.

Cameron opened the door, leaving it ajar while he combed through his kitchen for something to quiet his stomach. He'd give anything for a box of the muffins Lauren had put him on the plane with a few days ago. Instead he found a couple frozen meals. The microwave hummed to life, his dinner rotating on the glass turntable.

"You look awful. Who did that to your hair?"

Cameron didn't turn at the sound of Jeremy's voice. His cousin never failed to comment on how closely cropped he kept his hair.

"What is with you?" Jeremy crossed into the kitchen, leaning his dirty jean-clad hip against the counter and crossing his legs at the ankles.

"Take off your work boots. They're filthy." He kept his gaze firmly on the microwave.

"Man, you need to lighten up. Let's go out for a beer."

"I'm tired, Jer. Long week."

"Actually, it's a short week, with a holiday tomorrow."

"I'm not going to Aunt Dena's."

"Come on. I can't go if you don't go."

"How is that?" The microwave dinged. Cameron pulled down a plate and set the two steaming meals on it.

"Mom said I had to bring you. Period." Jeremy opened the fridge, pulling out two cans.

What did you know? He still had beer. "I'm going to stay here and catch up for my meetings on Friday."

"You financial freaks work the day after Thanksgiving?" Jeremy traded a meal for a beer and marched into the living room. Cameron followed, shaking his head when Jeremy plopped on the sofa and hoisted his heavy work boots onto the glass coffee-table.

"How is it you are gay, and I'm the one constantly re-minding you to take off your damned muddy shoes?"

Jeremy chucked his boots at the front door. "Why are you in such a foul mood?"

Cameron launched into a detailed explanation sure to bore his cousin into a coma. It felt good to recap the last week, helped to put everything in perspective.

"It's a woman, isn't it?"

"Have you heard a word I said? One of our main inves-tors filed bankruptcy, so I—"

"I heard you, Cam. But I know you. This work garbage doesn't faze you in the slightest. But women—one gets into your head and you're wrecked."

Before he could extol what an idiot Jeremy was, his cell phone chirped to life. Thankful for the reprieve, Cameron flipped it on without looking at the display.

"I've missed you." The suggestive voice purred through the phone.

Damn. Melinda Kramer. "How's Rob?"

"We broke up, sad story for another time. When can I see you?"

"I don't think that's a good idea, Mel." His conscience laughed at him. He and the sexy investment banker had a standing agreement to have sex, just sex, and nothing but sex whenever they were both unattached. An arrangement that had suited them well.

"I've been thinking about you for weeks. Imagine my disappointment when I found you'd moved to Seattle. But now you're here, and I'm here."

"I have plans with my family." He turned so he wouldn't have to see Jeremy's smug smile of victory.

"I'll work around that. I could come over right now. In an hour we could be sweaty and satisfied."

Best to nip this in the bud before it turned into phone sex, a favorite of Melinda's. "I'm with someone, Mel."

Her laugh was low and sinister. "You must be joking. You let some gold digger get her claws into you?"

"Goodbye, Mel."

"Cameron, wait. We've always been discreet. And the rule about not seeing other people was yours, not mine. I don't care what you do in Seattle, as long as you see me in New York."

"It's not a good idea, Mel. We can't see each other anymore. Goodbye." Cameron clicked off the phone and turned, the look on Jeremy's face making him cringe.

"You're with someone? Since when? Mel will find out you lied."

"It's not a lie. I am seeing somebody." He turned off his

phone to save himself the agony of explaining his and Lauren's arrangement. The calls from family would begin about two minutes after Jeremy left.

"Fine, you're seeing someone. Have you told her?"

"Melinda? You heard me tell her."

"No. Have you told your girlfriend what happened the last time you were in a relationship?"

Lauren stared at the bright red folders in her hands. She had poured every moment of the last few days into creating a business proposal to sway any investor. Budgets, menus, market research, timelines—everything mapped out except how her mother would react knowing she planned on focusing on business and not her relationship. Non-relationship. Whatever.

With a sigh she rocked back on her heels and looked up at the door. Her mother believed the woman stood behind the man, let her passions slide so his could shine. Cameron was successful enough to expect the same thing. She needed this to be there for her when he decided he wasn't interested anymore.

"I don't think I've ever seen you nervous before." Diego stood next to her, holding a bouquet of brightly colored flowers.

She'd never needed something this bad. Even starting Come For Dinner, she'd known if she failed she'd get past it. But getting past Cameron Price would take more of a safety net than her mother could provide. She'd need a reason to get up every day, people depending on her, too much to do so she wouldn't have time to think about what she'd lost. Only success was big enough to hide a heartache as big as that man was sure to deliver.

"Lauren, let's go in."

"Knock first." She swallowed, trying to buy more time. Her mother would see right through her.

"You knock at your mom's house?"

"Don't you?"

"No. And my mother lives in another country."

"Fine." Tucking the folders beneath her arm, Lauren reached into her lime-green handbag and gasped as her hand clutched her keys. The bag. Her mother would know she'd had retail therapy.

"What is with you?"

Think fast, Lauren. Never let anyone see you in a cold panic. "We should have brought dinner. A few of the prepared meals to give her an idea of what we have in mind."

"We should have brought casseroles? To Thanksgiving dinner with your mother? You know you sound crazy, right?"

"Right." Lauren nodded her head emphatically and slid the key in the lock. She needed to get a grip if she had any hope of her mother seeing this for the great opportunity it was.

The warm smell of roasting turkey and garlic butter wafted through the air as she stepped inside the house, stirring her confidence. Emma Brody loved food, loved creating healthy meals for people. She'd passed that love on to her daughter. Of course she'd want to spread it around.

"Mom? Where are you?" She opened the coat closet and hung up their coats, soft jazz music floating through the house.

"Just a minute, baby," Emma called from upstairs. Upstairs? She never went upstairs alone.

After a few quick seconds her mother appeared at the top of the stairway, a picture of modern elegance.

Slimming straight-leg black leather pants and a black cowl-neck sweater with sparkling metallic silver accents that set off the highlights in her gray hair.

"Mom, you look amazing." Lauren ran a hand over her cocoa and camel layered tissue tees and jeans and wished she'd remembered they used to dress for dinner.

"You look lovely, Mrs Brody." Diego smiled in his flat-front black trousers and black button-down. Even he'd thought to dress up.

"Diego, please, it's Emma." She descended the stairs with grace Lauren wished she'd inherited. "You're family to us. Let's go to the dining room. Anne and Michael are already there."

Lauren froze as her mother linked their arms. "You invited my staff? I thought it was just us. I wanted to discuss something with you."

"Anne still works here, remember? She's helped with the house since we bought it," Emma said with the smile of a perfect hostess. "I know you wanted to discuss something, but since you invited Diego I assumed it wasn't private."

"It is." Just what she needed, to be humiliated in front of the people she worked with every day.

"Lauren, everyone knows about your business proposal. I think it's a great idea. We can discuss it over dinner. Unless what you need to talk about is more personal?"

"No." She shook her head and opted to go with the flow. Couldn't fight fate, or Emma Brody.

"I wish Cameron could be here." Their arms locked, Emma pulled Lauren through the hall, Diego following closely behind. "I'd love to hear his opinions about your new venture."

Here it comes. "He's in New York on business. He

travels quite a bit." *So he won't take nearly as much of my time as you think he should.* She barely resisted the urge to stick out her tongue. She could do both, be the trophy and the career woman. At least for a while.

"He has a wonderful reputation for spotting new ventures. The finance community is quite taken with him already."

"Have you been asking about him?"

"Of course."

Arriving in the dining room, Lauren couldn't believe her eyes. The room had been completely redone. Twinkle lights sparkled from the two chandeliers, soft metallic fabrics draped the windows and doorway, small bouquets of white flowers sat on round mirrors down the center of the table, all giving the effect of a perfect winter evening.

"This is amazing, Mom." The decorations and the change in her, in the house. For so long empty and shut off, suddenly warm and inviting, surrounded by people. The way she remembered.

"I'm glad you like it. I'd forgotten how much I enjoyed entertaining until I saw the mirrors at the candle shop, and it all came together in my head."

"You went to a candle shop?" Lauren looked about the room, for the first time seeing the crystal candlesticks and silver tapers along the sideboard behind where Anne and her husband Michael sat.

"Malta Volk called to tell me what a wonderful job you did with the dinner at Cameron's last week, and she told me about this new place she's in love with. She said he's very handsome, by the way. I need to see for myself."

Not the subtlest of hints, but Lauren got the message. If Saturday went as she hoped, she'd have Cameron meet her mother. If not, they could stage an elaborate break-up scene at a party. She could only lie to her mother for so long.

Every spectacular dish on the Thanksgiving table tightened the knot of guilt. While the crew of Come For Dinner slaved away preparing traditional Thanksgiving fare for clients who no doubt passed it off as their own, a meal of restaurant quality was being prepared in their honor.

Brie-stuffed turkey breast, roasted red potatoes, broiled asparagus with garlic butter, and a delicate spinach salad with pomegranate seeds. The way the group talked over the proposal made the evening perfect, coming up with new and exciting ideas to set their venture apart. She'd never been more confident in the success of the project than when she waved goodbye to the guests and retreated to the large tiled kitchen to help her mother clean up.

Emma wiped down the counters as Lauren entered the room. She looked up with a sad smile. "You want to tell me something?"

"I think we covered everything but the legalities. Thank you again for backing our idea. Your support means everything."

Emma set the towel on the clean counter and leaned against it. "What am I supporting, Lauren? Defensive planning? Trying to make sure you can justify working too much because you have a new project in the works? Are you trying to sabotage your relationship? Or has it crashed already?"

"Mom, Cameron and I are complicated." The guilt threatened to poison her. What did it matter if one person knew?

"Are you in love with him, baby?"

"Yes." At least that wasn't a lie. She knew better than to be in love with him, but the heart wanted what it wanted.

"Then why would you want to start a new business now, when you need to be focused on your relationship with him?"

How did one explain the man you were in love with had no intention of actually falling in love with you?

Lauren hated that he'd kept her waiting. Life was short, best to rush to the good parts. Like sex with Cameron Price. Time for the final step in her plan to seduce him, the only part of this procedure she wasn't entirely comfortable with.

Lingerie made her nervous. She knew what a woman wore revealed intimate details about how she thought of herself. And she didn't want Cameron thinking she was plain cotton. Her outside persona was satin and lace. Her more private parts deserved the same kind of attention.

Before opening her underwear drawer this morning, Lauren had thought she had a decent collection of panties and pajamas. But looking at them as a man would, she'd been completely nonplussed. Sure, her nightgowns were trimmed with lace and in pretty colors, but they were knit jersey. All of them. Even her bras were boring, breathable, seamless.

She needed something that said, Don't you dare look away. Crossing the shopping center parking lot, she centered herself before entering the lingerie store. Women of all shapes and sizes milled around inside. Mannequins struck suggestive poses.

She set her jaw against the blush creeping up her shoulders. She was not a prude, damn it. She'd had sex before. Soon after her father and brother's funeral with the man she'd thought she'd marry and build a life around. A man who had soon let it be known his sexual appetites were not something she could fulfill alone.

Running away to Europe that summer to hide from her broken engagement, she'd had a drunken fling with an Italian who'd spoken no English. He'd made her realize why women raved about sex. She'd needed that affair to remind herself she was desirable, and to teach her what sex could be. Pleasurable, sure, but ultimately unfulfilling without an emotional connection.

A connection she had with Cameron, whether he reciprocated the sentiment or not. As she pushed open the doors to the boutique wafts of musky perfume assaulted her nose. Way to set the scene. Lauren stood up taller, hoping her approach would have a much more suggestive effect.

With a grin she approached the racks, fingering through the selections and trying to picture herself actually wearing a red silk babydoll that wouldn't even cover her panties. Which in this case would be a thong embroidered with sequins and beads to match the babydoll. Not her style, and yet she lifted the hanger from the rack and kept looking.

More outfits accumulated on her arm as she indulged her inner vixen. She'd spent every spare moment the past week designing the perfect seduction scene. Might as well reward them both for her labors. And if he held out on her again? Well, let him see a collection of all he'd missed out on hanging in his closet.

She experimented with fabrics, gathering lace, silk, satin, and sheer tulle. A different color for each of the half-dozen pieces she settled on. Having never tried the lingerie route before, she didn't know what would turn him on. Or her.

Next she selected bras more suited to a woman having an affair. Ladies who had affairs matched their bras and panties, so she bought everything in sets. Feeling every bit the seductress, she paid for her purchases, swinging the bags from her fingers as she tried not to skip to the car.

Halfway across the parking lot her cell phone began to buzz. Balancing the bags in one hand, she dug it out of her handbag. The number on the display had a New York area code. Hope swelled in her chest. She hadn't heard a word from him all week.

"Cameron?"

"No, Lauren," a woman's voice purred. "But I need to talk to you about Cameron."

CHAPTER TWELVE

THE house looked ominous in the evening twilight. Cameron hoped like hell Lauren had gotten his message about a later flight and having a taxi to take him home. He paid the driver and watched him drive away before sliding his key in the front door lock. The soft sounds of Vivaldi greeted him, alerting him to the fact that he wasn't alone. Setting his bags by the door, he crept slowly through the house, soaking up the changes.

The same white furniture sat in the living room, but the walls were now a rich chocolate brown. A warm beige enveloped the dining room, crimson candles flickering on the table. The leafy plants in the silvery pots were back, transforming the rooms from house to home.

He slid off his shoes and socks, digging his toes into the plush chenille rugs lining the hallway. Knowing Lauren was here, had done all this while thinking of him, caused a sudden surge of lust to charge through him.

He walked down the hall, pushing open the kitchen door. His jaw dropped at the sight before him. Lauren, wearing the sexiest dress he'd ever seen. Not that it was a dress really. At least not one he could handle her wearing with other people around. The sides of the black silk gown laced up like a corset, playing peek-a-boo with her curves. The front of the gown dipped dangerously low. With the low front and non-existent sides, he became painfully aware she wore nothing beneath it.

The unashamed honesty of her desire bewildered him. He felt it too, the chemistry electric in the room whenever they were together, but she knew he couldn't give her more than just an affair. She knew, and yet she courageously stepped into the flames for a chance to play with fire.

As he walked in she looked up from her work at the counter. The radiance in her sparkling eyes and bright smile eroded his resolve. Since the night they'd met he'd wanted her. And now, exhausted from a week of work and little sleep, he wanted nothing more than to let go of everything and take the risk. She'd gotten to him on every level but one. And he needed to remedy that immediately.

He closed the distance between them and captured her lips before she could say a word. Through his shirt he felt the heat of her hands clutching his arms while his mouth plundered hers. Her lips parted willingly, her sweet breath filling his mouth with the taste of ripe peaches.

Kissing Lauren was intoxicating. Had been since that first sizzling, powerful, overwhelming moment their lips had locked. A moment he'd been running towards ever since. He tugged at her lips, drawing a response from her so strong her fingernails dug into his arms.

Pulling his bottom lip between her teeth, she nipped hard enough for him to let her pull back.

"I knew it," she whispered, releasing him and pulling her bottom lip between her teeth as she turned back to the counter.

JENNA BAYLEY-BURKE   167

"Knew what?" For the first time he glanced at the counter strewn with platters of fruits and vegetables.

"You missed me."

"Guilty."

"Are you guilty, Cameron?" She looked up at him, her eyes asking a question he couldn't read. The expression vanished as quickly as it appeared. "Do you like your surprise?"

"The house looks amazing. So much warmer and more comfortable." He reached out, tracing a finger down the silken skin of her bare arm. His fingers toyed with the slippery strings holding her outfit together. One pull and it would all fall away.

"No." Lauren stepped away from him and circled the island in the center of the kitchen. She waved her hand over the top, gesturing to the platters. "First, you have to earn it. Anything you want, we'll do. As long as you eat it first."

The memory of her sweet taste flooded his mind and he took a step to follow her.

"Not me, the food."

Food, right. Taking a breath so deep his lungs hurt, he forced himself to focus on the platters on the countertop. His eyes widened.

"Did I ever tell you I was expelled from culinary school?"

He shook his head. Speaking now was impossible. She'd somehow worked fruits and vegetables into suggestively erotic presentations.

"We had to design a tablescape for a buffet. My theme proved too much for the instructors. But I don't think the effect is wasted on you."

Not in the slightest. Cameron's eyes drank in the sexual

smorgasbord. A banana carved in a suggestive shape. Two lemons tipped by cherries with a zucchini pressing between them. A yellow bell pepper sitting atop two celery stalks splayed with a pair of brussel sprouts below. And his favorite, another eggplant creation involving a peach and a yellow zucchini.

"Damn, that's hot."

"Makes you like vegetables, doesn't it?"

"I'll never look at eggplant the same way again, that's for sure."

"In art school I sold still photos to a men's magazine."

"Culinary school and art school?" he asked absent-mindedly, still trying to decide what to try first. He planned on sampling every dish.

"Plus I'm ten credits shy of my bachelor's degree."

He looked up in time to see the hesitancy in her gaze. "I'm surprised. I thought you finished whatever you started."

"Life is short. If it isn't worthwhile, I get out. No point in wasting time finishing if you've already learned what you meant to."

"You don't believe in commitment?" He arched a brow, wondering if he'd read her wrong.

"I don't believe in staying in a destructive situation just because you committed to it. My father and brother died, and I ended an engagement right before I finished college and I needed some space to think. When I came back I tried culinary school, but that didn't work out, and then art school until I came up with the plan for catering."

"You were engaged to the guy who cheated on you?" Somehow, that made the blow all the more devastating. Nearly as bad as what had happened to him.

Her lip quivered as she nodded.

"What did you do?"

"Cam, I'd rather you picked a dish." Her chest hitched with her ragged breath.

"I'd rather know what happened."

"His mother sued me." Her smile reappeared and he knew she'd found an angle to play. A way to evade him. Unless she showed him hers, he'd never be able to confess his. "She wanted damages for canceling the wedding. So I ran away to Europe for the summer and let him explain everything to his mother."

So she didn't want to strip away the layers and be intimate, only physical. If she didn't trust him with her past, she didn't think they had a future. The realization should have calmed him, but he found it irksome.

Not that he'd been more forthcoming.

"Cameron?" While he'd been lost in thought she'd moved to stand in front of him. "Do you see anything you want to try?"

He blinked, trying to focus on the task at hand instead of being rueful. He drummed his fingers on the counter-top, wondering where to start.

"Wait a minute." Cameron cupped her face in his hands and pressed his lips to hers. A short, wet kiss that confirmed his suspicions. "You've been eating peaches. And the only peach—" he moved his hand to his favorite option, one that would have her legs in the air so he could watch the show "—is right here. And I do love peaches."

"That's fine. But there is zucchini and eggplant on that plate too."

"You wicked girl." He scanned the plethora of erotically styled food again. "Everything for you is a fruit, and everything for me is a vegetable."

"Not completely. There is the banana."

Cameron picked up the banana, intent on calling her bluff. But part of him couldn't bring himself to put it in his mouth. "I'm never going to be able to eat a banana again."

"Then you'll have no use for an ice-cream maker."

"So you'll be eating peaches regularly?"

"Cameron!"

"I'll make you a deal, I'll eat your peach if you eat my banana." He handed her the fruit, biting his cheek to keep from laughing.

"Fine. You have me there." She spun on her heel and marched to the other side of the kitchen, sliding on oven mitts and pulling an oblong pan from the oven. He watched as she scooped the dish onto a plate and slid open a drawer for a fork, shutting it with her hip.

"What is this?" He stared down at the plate of what resembled macaroni and cheese studded with red, green, yellow, and purple.

"Your dinner."

He groaned. "I want you now. But I had a bagel for breakfast and nothing since."

Her laughter echoed through the room as she stepped closer and wrapped her arms around his waist. "Then you should eat whatever you want."

"And I have a confession to make."

"You do?" She stepped back, wrapping her arms around herself.

"I'll eat pretty much anything. I'm not as picky as you think I am, I simply get caught up with working and forget to eat." He plucked the strawberry from between the splayed eggplant legs for effect, catching her smile.

"You're not picky?"

"No. I just don't want people I'm working with concentrating on crumbs on my shirt instead of what I have to say."

"Well, then, I wouldn't want to be distracted from what you have to say tonight."

Creamy macaroni warmed his mouth, but he was too distracted to taste much of anything as Lauren began to undress him with exaggerated slowness. Her fingers rubbed at his wrist as she undid the buttons on his cuffs, tickled his chest as she popped open the ones on his shirt. She pulled his shirt from his trousers and reached for his belt.

His hand covered hers. "Did you bring condoms?"

"I've done all this, and you didn't even buy condoms?"

He'd told her repeatedly he had no time for a relationship. He only thought about it when his world slowed, usually right before drifting off at night. Not exactly peak shopping hours.

"My pants should stay on, then. But your dress should come off." Setting down his fork, he reached for the peach and bit into it.

Lauren wrapped her arms around him, licking his lips where a droplet of peach nectar had dribbled. His free hand followed the silken cord across her side, pressing into the warm, smooth flesh and over her rounded backside.

"You're not wearing any panties, are you?"

Her curls swished as she shook her head. "I bought condoms. They're up in your room. But, I got my birth-control shot on Tuesday so we're good to go."

He set the peach down on the counter, surveying the plates. Plucking a cherry half from one platter, he popped it into his mouth and turned back to her. "Lemons."

"Lemons?" Her long eyelashes fluttered as she blinked.

Through the thin silk of her gown he pinched her beaded nipple until she gasped. He pushed the strap from her shoulder, pinning her arm to her side and baring her ripe breast. Taking a lemon half from the platter, he squeezed the citrus against her chest, licking up every drop of tart juice before it reached her dress.

The plum from the tip of the zucchini came next. He rubbed the fruit down her neck, kissing at the stickiness until he could taste her flesh. His hands worked to undo the sides of her dress, until it fell with a whoosh at their feet.

"You make me so hungry, Lauren." With the last vestiges of his self-control he framed her face in his hands and stared into her eyes, now heavy-lidded with lust. "Are you sure you can do this?"

Her answer was a confident, knowing gaze that tickled at his soul. A look that proved their being together was a physical inevitability. A when, not an if. But if he was letting her see more of his soul than he intended, he could see this wasn't just sex for her either. The vibrancy of her fantasy seeped around them, made him feel she didn't simply want to act out her desires, but she wanted to act them out with him.

He grabbed her wrist and pulled her across the room to the kitchen table. She wrapped her arms around his neck, giggling as he grasped her waist and lifted her onto the table. He silenced the girlish sound with his mouth, reminding her she was all woman.

Hands flitted about, peeling off the rest of his clothes at record speed so they could be bare together, except for her high-heeled sandals. They looked hot, and he doubted he could figure out how to get them off.

She massaged his pectoral muscles with her palms, her fingernails tracing the indentation of muscle on his shoulders, chest, and stomach. Her touch was soft and tentative, but he needed more. Much more.

Pulling her against him, he lined up their bodies, pressing his need against her so she'd know how out of control she made him. His hands on her were hard and demanding. He'd been dreaming of her warm and willing beneath him all week. Now that he had the chance he was like a kid in a candy store, filling himself with everything at once.

She wrapped her arms around his neck and gave him the control he needed. With his hand at the small of her back he moved her where he wanted her, kissing every inch of her body within reach. He nibbled across her jaw, nipped at her earlobe, placed butterfly kisses down her long neck, a long, slow lick at the base of her throat. When he blew across her damp skin she shuddered, spreading her legs wider to rock her sex against his.

His hands roved over her breasts, learning what to do to make her writhe and sigh. Her ripe nipples were too much of an invitation to ignore, so his mouth engulfed them, licking and sucking until she began to moan and rock her heat against him faster.

A few more seconds of that and it would be over for both of them. He stepped back just enough to relieve the torturous pressure and looked into her beautiful green eyes, his gaze dropping to her lips, swollen from his kisses, breasts moist and nipples puckered from his attention, to the sparse thatch of blonde hair hiding the secrets between her legs.

His fingers began to work teasingly at her moist center, spreading her wetness over her swollen clitoris. Circling the bud of nerves with one finger, he traced her nether lips from the top to just below her entrance. He knelt down and parted her lips, his breath tickling her flesh. Slowly, he slid a finger inside, waiting for her to relax before adding another.

Working an unhurried rhythm with his fingers, he

leaned closer, running his tongue along her at the same time. She gasped, her hands clenching the edge of the table. To steady her he propped her legs over his shoulders and settled in.

"I'm supposed to seduce you." She bucked against him, taking her pleasure through her protests.

"I could stop." He peeked up at her, desire flashing in her bright eyes.

"No!" One hand pushed his head back to his task, the other reaching for the far side of the table. Her nails scratched at his scalp as he began flicking figure eights across her clitoris. She breathed words he didn't take the time to decipher. Something about not liking his hair so short.

He lifted her bottom off the table and flattened his tongue against her sex, licking up and down to the tempo his fingers set. Soft breathy moans became the muted screams of climax. She clenched around his fingers as the surge of satisfaction washed over her body.

He could see the muscles of her stomach quiver with the remnants of her orgasm. Proof of pleasure that couldn't be faked. He loved the volcanic passion he could coax from her.

Before she recovered completely he stood, taking his place between her legs. He grasped her hips to center her and pushed her knees to her shoulders. Sliding the pad of his thumb over the bud of her clitoris, he smiled as she opened her eyes. The tip of his rock-hard penis replaced his thumb and he explored every inch of her, covering himself in her wetness.

"You want me to beg, don't you?" She squirmed in her prone position, pulling her bottom lip between her teeth as she caught sight of their joining. "Damn. You're even bigger than last time."

Modesty had no place here. "You turned me on even more with that orgasm."

"My coming makes you—" She gasped as he eased himself inside.

"Relax," he whispered. He pushed himself inside her with gentle insistence, waiting for her to gradually accept his penetration. With a final thrust he buried himself inside her, a move that brought his name to her lips. She arched into him, and he caught her knees on his forearms.

Locking her into place, a feeling pure and raw came over him. Absolute nirvana. He pulled back and then filled her with long, slow strokes, enjoying every delicious inch of pleasure.

"I can barely move," she said breathlessly.

She moaned, the faint blush of desire blooming across her glistening chest. He picked up speed, watching their joining with building excitement. Her head rolled back and she cried out in rapturous surrender.

He matched her sounds of pleasure with his own, a perk to living in a house instead of an apartment he'd never considered. Complete privacy. He could take her on the back lawn and no one would know. On the deck, in the hot tub, in front of the fireplace, on the weight bench, the shower. Dear God, the possibilities were endless.

As each scene flashed through his mind he pumped faster, harder, his excitement building. Her legs straightened, her feet finding his shoulders. The change in position moved him impossibly deeper, and allowed him the use of a hand.

Her normally sweet and breathy voice turned scratchy and throaty from shouting and the sound heightened his pleasure. As did watching her grip the opposite edge of the table, her breasts bouncing with his every thrust. He reached up and pinched her nipple, pulling and twisting until she screamed.

She was tossing her pale curls from side to side at a frantic pace, and he knew she had to be close. And so was he. Her legs went slack, falling from his shoulders onto his forearms a second before he felt her tighten around his shaft. Hair covered her face, so he couldn't see her, but he heard hitches in her breath, felt the spasmodic pulsing deep inside. But what pushed him over the edge was the sound of his name on her tiny pants of breath.

He had to lean against the table as the climax rocked through his body, turning to the colors of a vibrant sunset behind his closed eyes. His entire body warmed, from his scalp to his toes and everywhere in between. He'd known sex with Lauren would be good, but this was life-affirming.

When the roaring in his ears stopped and he wasn't chasing every breath, he stood up. Releasing her legs, he slid from her body. She made no move, legs dangling over the table edge. In fact, she didn't stir at all.

"Lauren?" He ran a hand up her body, slick with sweat. No response. "Baby?"

His voice held a tremor he didn't recognize. His heart thudded in his ears until she began to stretch her lithe body like a cat.

"Are you okay?"

"Mmm-hmm." She kept stretching, her arms over her head, her toes pointing.

"Let's go upstairs and try the shower." He reached for her arm, but she still stretched.

"Not yet. I'm still rippling."

"Rippling?" *What in the world?*

"Waves and then wakes, then ripples. You are amazing. I've never rippled with a man before."

He loved the way she gave words her own meaning. "How do you usually ripple?"

"I'll show you if you ever stay at my place." With a sigh she sat up, reaching her arms overhead with a yawn. "I think we just hit the glass ceiling on sex. Wow."

Her delicious grin deserved a kiss. Nibbling at her lips, he stayed far enough away to whisper against her mouth, "We can do better. Imagine if you could move."

"Oh." She wrapped her arms around his neck and giggled. "I think I'd die if it got better. But that's how I want to go, so I'm game."

She slid her body against his as her feet found the floor and she stood, clutching him for support. Her eyes sparked with fire as she looked up at him.

"Didn't you say something about a shower?"

"Cam? Are you sleeping?" Lauren whispered in the dark, tugging the blanket higher on her shoulder.

"I'm rippling. Who knew?" He laughed, turning towards her. "I think I'm done for the night."

"Me too. I can't sleep." She reached between them, taking his hand. "Who's Melinda Kramer?"

Cameron sat up so fast his hand jerked from hers. He flipped on the bedside lamp and turned back to her. "What?"

"She called me." Lauren squinted until her eyes adjusted to the light, then found his hand again, holding it tighter this time.

"What did she say to you?" Anger laced his voice.

"She said you went to New York to be with her." Lauren propped herself up on one elbow.

"I didn't even see her. Why in the world would she call you?"

"Some nonsense about wanting me to know my boyfriend came with a mistress in New York."

"But I—" Her finger on his lips silenced him.

"I know, Cam. I'm not accusing you of anything. You're not exactly an easy lay."

"What does that mean?" A muscle twitched in his jaw.

"I painted your house to get into your pants. I doubt some other woman could do better." She traced a finger along his tense arm. "I didn't believe her. I just need to know if she's jealous, or crazy."

"I don't…I didn't…" Cameron rubbed his hands over his face and let out a frustrated groan. "I haven't seen her in a year at least, since she got engaged. We had an understanding that whenever we were single, we'd…I don't like talking to you about this." Cameron bolted from the bed, marching into the bathroom.

That was not in the script. Lauren threw off the covers and marched right after him. Realizing she was naked, she pulled the chenille throw from the foot of the bed and wrapped it around her body. Satisfied she'd covered anything he could use to distract her, she pushed open the bathroom door.

Cameron stood at the sink, a glass of water in hand. He caught her gaze in the mirror and shook his head. "I'll talk to her. She won't bother you again."

Lauren shook her head. "I don't think you should contact her at all. If she's dangerous, you should get a restraining order. If she's trying to get a rise out of you, it's best to ignore her completely."

"I can't just let her harass you." He put the glass down and turned. "You didn't sign on for that."

"I agreed to be a fake girlfriend for one night. Anything beyond that has been my choice." Lauren stepped closer, taking his hand and tugging him towards her. "I didn't mean to upset you. I was worried she might be nuts."

"She wanted to resume things while I was in New York."

"I can't blame her. You are amazing." She let go of his hand and unwrapped the throw, crawling back into bed and pulling the covers around her.

"That doesn't upset you?" Cameron shut off the bathroom light and leaned against the doorway, blissfully naked.

"Dating a sex god? Can't see the downside." Lauren snuggled into her pillow.

All at once Cameron was on top of her, using the blankets to keep her from moving. His vibrant blue eyes stared down at her. "Aren't you worried?"

Lauren shook her head. "If you wanted her, you would have had her."

"You know I didn't?"

"A woman knows." She closed her mouth to keep her lip from trembling and giving her away, but by the way his expression softened she knew he'd seen it.

"How did you know?"

"You still kiss the same."

Cameron looked at her for a long moment, then shifted to his side of the bed and shut off the lamp, crawling beneath the blankets. "I don't think it works that way."

"Not if the guy's been cheating since the beginning. But otherwise, it's a good barometer."

Lauren listened to the rhythm of his breath, using it to calm herself to sleep.

"From the beginning?" The lines of his face hardened,

and she felt him pondering. If that was what had happened to him, he'd never felt the difference.

"If they were never really with you from the start, then nothing would change."

"Sometimes I read these articles in magazines," Cameron said just before she drifted off. "And I'll try things. Just to see."

"It's not a technique, it's the feeling behind it that changes," she mumbled, trying not to yawn. "Let me know if there is something you read for me. I find fun stuff all the time. Like this article on what underwear says about your relationship." She couldn't hold back the yawn. "It had me spending way too much time in a lingerie boutique."

"You bought lingerie?" Cameron scooted closer, placing a hand on her bare thigh.

"You saw some of it earlier."

"Thank goodness. I though that was a dress." He chuckled, tucking her head beneath his chin and drifting off to sleep.

CHAPTER THIRTEEN

"IS THAT a dress?" Couln't be. But why was she coming out of the kitchen wearing lingerie ten minutes before the guests arrived?

"It's vintage designer, if you can believe it." Lauren turned from loading CDs in the stereo. "And from your expression, I can tell the importance is lost on you. Trust me, the other wives will be impressed."

"It's really short." And low cut, with a sparkling pendant drawing attention to just how low the gauzy fabric dipped between her breasts.

"You're telling me." She returned to her work on the stereo. "I couldn't wear the thigh-highs I planned, so I'm stuck with pantyhose, and I hate pantyhose." She turned back around with a smile, but her face fell instantly. "You don't like it?"

She nervously smoothed her hands down the black crepe of the draped pleats. Guilt crept in. She looked amazing. From the low pony-tail she'd coaxed her hair into, to the dress, to the sparkling heels on her feet. And bright red toenail polish. That hadn't been there last night.

"I'd like the dress better if we were alone." Stepping to

her, Cameron placed a hand on the textured material at her hip, grazing her cheek with a kiss.

Her smile showed her relief. After all she'd done for him, he didn't want to make her self-conscious. Thanks to jet lag he hadn't woken before her, so he'd opened his eyes to a note detailing her busy day. Somehow, she and her team had managed to cater a retirement luncheon, deliver three prepared dinners, and set this party up.

"Promise me you'll eat tonight, Cam."

He thought about pointing out he ate last night, but didn't want to steer the conversation down a road they couldn't travel with a dozen people about to descend on their privacy, and another handful in the kitchen.

With a sigh, Lauren turned on the stereo and stepped to the dining room, now warm and inviting with rich earth tones everywhere. The sounds of a demanding orchestra opened, fading to opera.

"I'm not a big fan of opera." Cameron's lip curled and he thought about changing her music selection. Would have done if there'd been investors coming tonight. But since the guests included a hydroelectric lobbyist, wind-power aficionado, two junior partners from the firm, and an environmental journalist, he knew he didn't have to impress. They had to impress him.

"Opera isn't a favorite of mine either. We're going Italian tonight, though, so it fits." Lauren grabbed a bowl of grapes, setting a bunch in front of each place setting and nestling a name card between the grapes.

She seemed more comfortable in his house than him. Where did she expect things to go with them? He knew she'd stepped into the agreement for her business, but if he could keep her interested in him with sex, all the better.

Because he was beginning to realize he felt something more for her.

Not the scars of suspicion and jealousy that usually kept him from investing too much in a relationship, but a comfortable playfulness he'd always envied in others. A compatibility and understanding he'd never known. He warned himself not to get too used to it. Like every other woman who traded up for a bigger fish in the sea, she would move on to the next man who could do more for her.

Except, he had more money now than ever before, and in a few years he'd be running a venture-capital firm with the best record in the country. Tamping down the wave of insecure speculation, he vowed to do what she'd asked. Try them out and see where it went.

Cameron leaned against the entry and watched Lauren and her team flutter about the room. Laying a brown runner down the center of the mossy green tablecloth and putting small bowls of olives with curls of lemon peel on top. Next came two baskets of artisan breads with sprigs of rosemary tucked between. Diego emerged from the kitchen, decorating the wet bar near the entry with bottles of wine, a large salami, red grapes, and wedges of cheese.

He didn't know how to feel about Diego, about any man working so closely with a woman as stunning as Lauren and not considering taking more from her. But then, he worked with women and never thought of them as such. Maybe Diego saw Lauren the same way.

"Did you buy her that dress?" Diego asked once Lauren had disappeared into the kitchen. He didn't look up, too busy arranging the salami.

"No. She says it's vintage and the other wives will like

it. I say it's too damned short." Cameron stepped to the entry table and poured himself a glass of wine.

"She never usually dresses like that," Diego said next to him, adding a clear vase filled with skinny breadsticks to the arrangement.

"It's a classy dress, there's just not much too it," said Cameron.

"You're right. I never see this side of her, so it shocked me."

"Do you want to see this side of her?" He had to know. Just because there was nothing on Lauren's side, that didn't mean the man wouldn't become a problem later.

He actually laughed. "I'm not a masochist. We work well together, but beyond that we'd be disastrous. She always has to be right. And in control. Every second of her day is planned so she can get the most done. It exhausts me to look at her sometimes." Diego gathered his empty bags. "I wish you luck."

"I need it. Turns out she can't be with a man who doesn't own an espresso machine and an ice cream maker. Do you know where I'd get those?"

What a boring clutter of people. Absolutely no interesting flirt factor. The lobbyist couple was almost predatory in their attentions to the other guests, and it put a pall over her party. She'd told Cameron not to invite them.

Trying to revive the night with tiramisu, Lauren flitted about the room like a butterfly, trying to keep each swirl of conversation light, fun, and on task.

Everyone enjoyed the dessert, her specialty thank-you, very much, but the lobbyist leering at her, and the other wives looking at her like some kind of high-maintenance trophy, had Lauren escaping to the kitchen for a breather.

"What a night." She leaned against the spotless countertop and watched her crew packing the items they'd finished with. "I swear, it was like trying to keep a campfire going in a rainstorm. The second I walked away from a group all conversation stopped. And this creep Cameron invited won't keep his hands to himself."

Anne snickered and sat in a kitchen chair. "It's the dress."

"You like it?" She twirled for effect. "I borrowed it from my mom's closet."

"Every man in that room liked it, so much so their tongues hung out of their mouths when you walked away. Their wives had to slap them to stop the drooling." Anne tapped a finger against her wrinkled cheek.

Lauren sat in the chair next to Anne and lowered her voice. "Come on. Surely this dress isn't that scandalous."

"It's gorgeous. And so are you. You're also a good decade younger than any other woman in that room. The husbands didn't want to say the wrong thing, and the wives didn't want to say anything at all."

"That's so…archaic." Lauren wrinkled her nose and smoothed her hands against the skirt of the dress.

"Some people never evolve."

Abruptly, the music piping through the house shut off. Muffled voices from the living room sounded strained. Anxiety coursing through her, Lauren returned to her guests, watching as they collected their coats at the door.

"Why is everyone leaving?" she asked discreetly the wife of one Cameron's employees.

"Cameron said he wasn't feeling well and the party was over, then he went upstairs."

Lauren ushered the guests out of the house as quickly

as she could, annoyed that the couple who had upset the swirl of her party waited for last to leave.

"We'd love to have you over for dinner." The wife reached out and touched her face, making Lauren take a step back.

"We're really quite busy with work and the holidays right now. I need to make sure Cameron is all right." She opened the door wider, and waved her hand in suggestion they get out of her house.

"I'm sorry if we upset you both." The lobbyist started in as Lauren tried to close the door. The back of his hand brushed against her bare arm and she stepped part way behind the door. It was one thing to shrug off his too familiar touches for the sake of a smooth party, but if he laid a hand on her again she'd slam it in the heavy steel door.

"It's been a long night. If you'll excuse me." She slammed the door, wanting to open it just to slam it again in their faces. What had the man implied to Cameron that had him bailing on his own party?

She'd promised. Cameron shook his head, realizing her hormone-driven promise held as much weight as the flimsy curtains blowing in the frigid December breeze. He could still hear the murmur of voices downstairs, the clatter of decorations being packed and carried away. It took all he had not to sneak out the garage and go for a good long run.

As he sank down onto the bed his aching head fell into his hands. He'd known better than to try for more than casual. Her empty promise couldn't shield him from the reality he'd witnessed. He'd been blind to it the first time, but he wouldn't be in that situation ever again.

He'd noticed the other men's appreciative glances, but had felt proud, not threatened, had found it amusing she never seemed to notice the way men looked at her.

Until he'd seen red. The lobbyist hadn't seemed able to keep his hands to himself, and Lauren had done nothing to brush him away. Cameron knew better than to open himself up to this.

He wasn't ready to put a label on what he felt for her, but he did care for her more than he should. Until tonight he'd thought she felt the same way. So many things she'd said and done added up to make him think she was open to the possibility of more, should he give her the slightest hint he'd be agreeable to it.

"Are you okay?" Lauren's voice tried to break into his thoughts.

Cameron said nothing, willing her to disappear and praying for the strength to let her go before he got in any deeper.

"What happened?" She stepped closer, putting a hand on his shoulder. He flinched, shifting out of her reach. He looked up at her, praying she couldn't see the painful yearning he felt for her in his gaze. Uncertainty flickered briefly in Lauren's green eyes.

Taking a breath to steady himself, Cameron looked her in the eye. "I can't do this, Lauren. You need to leave."

"No." She crossed her arms across her chest, intensity etched on her face. "Tell me what happened." She kept her distance and her protective stance.

He wanted her to leave. Knew she would bolt as soon as he confronted her with what he'd seen, so he hit her with it. "I saw you with him."

"I didn't—"

Cameron shook his head and tapped his temple. "I saw you. The way you flirted tonight, saw their hands on you. You never once brushed them off."

"I didn't want to make a scene."

"Unless it's what you wanted. To draw their attention, catch a bigger fish?"

"You're jealous."

"Maybe I'm just seeing you for what you are. Moving up, looking for a better deal."

"If you really believe that, I will go."

She leveled her gaze at him, chastising him with a glare. In light of what he'd seen, from her tonight and women who'd left before, he knew better than to trust her. Which was the real reason he couldn't have more than a relationship in passing. After that night, he'd learned not to trust anyone but himself.

"This isn't about tonight, is it?"

He closed his eyes. The scenes in his mind changing from imaginary to vicious memories. His stomach reeled and his mind went blessedly blank.

"What happened?"

"When your ex told you he'd found someone else, what did you do?"

"I ran away to Europe for the summer."

"No, not after. What did you do in that moment?"

Her mouth moved, but no words came. He watched the pain cross her face before she swallowed and spoke. "I froze. I heard the words, and I saw what I would become if I accepted it and married him. I flashed to my brother and my father's funeral and thought this was the only good thing about them being gone. If they hadn't died I wouldn't have postponed the wedding, and I wouldn't have slept with him because I felt empty, and I wouldn't have known any of it until it was too late."

She reached up and wiped her eyes of tears she refused to let fall. She'd resolved never to cry about it again. Sobbing got her nothing but puffy eyes. She met Cameron's gaze and held it, seeing his secret was far darker than hers.

"I opened the door and saw her, and him, in my bed. She still had my ring on. But his father was a millionaire, so I should understand her choice. It was never me she wanted, but who she thought I would become."

"Was that the only time?" The cold pain of his devastation was warmed by the realization he trusted her. His jealousy could only mean she wasn't alone in investing emotions into this relationship.

"That a woman used me? No. Just the last time I let anyone rub my nose in it."

"And that's what you thought I was doing tonight? Trawling in front of your face?"

"Weren't you?"

With a groan Lauren wrenched her arms behind her, unzipping the dress and shrugging it off. When it hit her feet she stepped out and kicked it at his face. Clad only in pantyhose and heels, she squared her shoulders and stared at him.

"This dress is obviously too much for us to handle right now. I wore it because I wanted your attention. Instead, I got the attention of some idiots, and you on the verge of accusing me of something we both know I'm not doing."

She reached for his cheek and he closed his eyes when she touched his skin. "How you reacted is perfectly normal to me. We don't know where this is going, so we think outrageous things to try and protect ourselves. I wear designer dresses to try to fit in with the other wives and show you we can be more than temporary, and you think because some idiots in your past traded up I will too."

"Don't make excuses for me, Lauren. The urge to stop myself from being hurt is so strong, it's primal. I don't want to hurt you because of it."

"There is only once choice I can see." She slid her hands around his neck, slipping down beside him on the bed. "Indulge your primal urges with me."

CHAPTER FOURTEEN

CAMERON had never thought someone would be this accepting and understanding. The challenge in Lauren's gaze calmed him in ways nothing else could. A peaceful certainty that as long as he was with Lauren, he'd never have to worry about reliving that moment.

"At first I wanted to throw my glass of wine at him, but with the white carpets in this mausoleum, that would become my headache, not his. So I thought about you and me in the shower." Her lips brushed against his softly. "About lemons and zucchini and plums and strawberries."

He cupped her cheeks with his hands and kissed her face off. How in the world had he ever gotten so lucky to find her, this woman who'd accept everything about him without judgment or reprimand? And how had he missed it until now?

"I'll be back in an hour," he said, stepping away and grabbing his shirt and shoes from the floor.

"You're leaving, right now?" Lauren's pink lips formed a perfect moue. "Where are you going?"

"To do something I should have done a week ago."

* * *

New York had its advantages, with theaters he never had time to go to, and restaurants he chose based on clients' requests. But New York City did not have super centers. Places like this one where you could buy a Christmas tree, tree stand, twinkle lights, a tablecloth to swirl around the base, an espresso machine, and an ice-cream maker with one swipe of a credit card. Even better, the staff had found his rushed shopping spree so amusing they had helped him collect the ingredients for chocolate ice cream and tied the tree to the top of his car.

Cameron parked by the kitchen door, deciding to set up the tree in the den rather than the living room. He pushed all the furniture to the side of the room and set up the tree in the middle, so they could see both the fireplace and the tree if they lay on the floor. His and hers fantasies at their best.

He set up the tree exactly as they had told him at the store, trying not to get tangled in the tiny lights as he wound them around. He draped the tablecloth around the base to cover it up and brought in the food and appliances in the oversized gift bags he'd purchased. Setting them at the base of the tree, he felt like Santa Claus. Well, Santa minus fifty pounds.

Dashing up the stairs for a quick shower, he checked the rooms for Lauren. Finally he found her asleep on his bed. She'd stretched out on top of the white comforter, her make-up washed off and her hair around her shoulders. A paperback lay open next to her hand.

The vision of Lauren on his bed in sage-green silk tap pants trimmed in lace and a sheer-lace-trimmed camisole that exposed her taut belly gave him pause. This must be part of the lingerie collection she'd promised. He'd need to be more creative with his gifts to keep up with presents like this.

He didn't want to wake her before his shower, but curiosity about what she read had him gently lifting the book from the bed. He closed the door on the bathroom before turning on the light and flipping through the pages. From what he skimmed about tropical locations and hot, sticky skin, he knew it was romance. But the scene with the warmed honey had him deciding on a very cold shower, and praying she'd gotten that far in the book.

After drying off and changing into a pair of black silk boxers he set the book on the nightstand and sat on the bed beside her. His finger against the skin of her arm elicited a smile.

"Did you like what you read?" She spoke without opening her eyes.

"You're not asleep?"

"I'm drifting in and out. Did you read the bit about eating pasta off his chest? I'm not doing that."

One would hope not. "Did you read the part about the honey?"

"No." She sat up and looked around, her gaze catching the book on the nightstand. "Would you read it to me?"

"Like a bedtime story?"

"Yes, please." She sat up on her knees. "I'll even promise to buy honey."

"Okay." He wondered how comfortable he'd be reading the suggestive words aloud. But then it was Lauren, and, if it upped his odds of having her lick warm honey off his penis, he was game. He shifted as the mental picture came into focus. "But first I have something downstairs for you."

"I told you, I bought condoms." Lauren leaned across

the bed, pulling open the drawer to showcase her display of colorful packages.

Good thing, because he hadn't even thought of that while he'd been out. "It's better than condoms." He stood, tugging her to her feet.

He led her down the stairs, ignoring her questions of where he'd gone and protests about buying her things. Down the dark hallway he pulled her behind him, flipping the switch in the den that turned on the lights for the tree.

She gasped and clutched his hand tighter, her other hand on her chest. "My tree!"

He gave her hand a squeeze, then released it, crossing the room to flip the switch that lit the gas fireplace. The room had a soft warm glow, flickering with the firelight and the festive scent of pine.

The only things in the room he could throw on the ground were the white chenille throws from the white couches. Lauren and her bursts of color hadn't made it into this room yet. He spread the blankets between the tree and the fireplace and sat, reaching for the gift bags.

"I asked Diego where to buy what you wanted, but he said I needed to let you order them for yourself, no matter what you said." He looked up at her, glassy eyed and still standing by the entryway. "Come on, prove him wrong."

She stepped to the edge of the blankets and kneeled down, tucking her strawberry-blonde hair behind her ears. "You and Diego talked about me?"

"A little." He nudged the bag closer. "He said you'd want industrial-sized machines that you had to order from catalogs for parties. But this is for now."

She squealed when she lifted the ice-cream maker from the bag, so he slid her the heavier bag. A peal of laughter rang through the room as she ripped away the side of the bag to see the espresso machine. He passed her another bag, which did not have the same effect.

She put her gifts aside and closed her eyes, a teardrop squeezing out of each eye. "I can't do this."

His heart stalled in his chest, tightening until he remembered to breathe.

"I'm breaking the rules. I know I promised you I could do this, just be physical and have no strings, but I can't. Especially when you do things like this."

She wiped her eyes with the back of her hand and continued. "I thought I could, that I was too restless for commitment, too independent for a relationship. But I can't pretend I'm not crossing the line and it's just an intellectual fascination or a physical attraction anymore. I haven't had to fake any of it, even though I know it isn't real."

"It's real to me." He scooted closer to her, taking her trembling hand in his. "I think we've caught up to where people assumed we were from the beginning."

"Really?" She wiped her eyes again and sniffed, letting out a long slow breath.

"I never thought I'd find someone strong enough to support me without dragging me down. A person who cared about me and not my income potential." She wiped at her eyes again. "Please stop crying. It makes me want to do something to make you feel better."

"So, make me feel better." Lauren reached for him, touching him differently than before. With more need and less hunger. His skin was so soft and strong beneath her hands as she reached around him, caressing his shoulders and back. She rubbed her hands down his sides, to the elasticized band keeping his boxers on.

His lips tantalized her as they began to kiss, his tongue stoking the fire inside of her. She hungered for his long-fingered caress, the completeness of having him inside of her.

He pulled away and framed her face in his hands, staring into her eyes. At the sight of his hypnotic gaze she wanted to say it. *I love you.* Wanted to say the words from her soul and not as a conciliation or replacement for goodbye over the telephone. For once she knew the power of the words.

But they caught in her throat. She'd pushed him so far already tonight. Yesterday their game had still been on for him. Best not to rock the boat until he had his sea legs under him.

"Look at me," he whispered, the vulnerability in his voice melting her.

"I am."

His head shook slightly. "You're zoning out. I want to look at you."

Her breath quickening, she gave herself over to his request. When he looked at her that way, she thought he could see her soul. Let him see the truth there, then her love for him wouldn't come as a surprise later.

Energy surged between them, the emotions flowing from one to the other and back again until they felt the same thing. Lauren felt them merging, though they barely touched, her body tingling with the desire in his. The notes of a simple melody danced across her skin, a song she knew he played in his head.

A thrilling rush of adrenaline shot through her, piquing all her senses. She looked deep into his beautiful soul, saw the tears there that had left him broken and lonely. She saw what needed healing and knew she could.

She also saw confirmation of what she'd felt earlier at his confession. He'd learned from his mistakes. She looked deeper, seeing the man who wanted to use his position to save the world from itself. Altruistic capitalism.

What he tried to hide as his eyelids grew heavy rocked her to the core. She felt his love for her. Maybe it was hopeful, or her own affection mirrored back to her in his eyes. But she didn't doubt it, let it in and flow through her with a powerful gush. And then the power left her in a turbulent pull. Her eyes widened at the shock, her body pulsing as vibrant colors danced around them.

She fell forward against him, her sex clenching in tiny spasms. Her heart thundered in her chest, her body taut as a live wire. Had he really brought her to climax without touching her?

"I've read about that," he whispered against her hair, his hand rubbing slow circles on her back. "That night on the piano, I thought we might be able to, and it scared me."

"What is it?"

"Tantric. Minds connecting."

She looked up at him. "Did you?"

"Not yet. We'll get the timing down with practice." His lips dropped down to meet hers in a soft kiss. He pulled her body closer to his, then broke the kiss to lift the chemise over her head.

He laid her down beside him and she gave herself permission to enjoy him without worries of sexual equality or tomorrow. Her body already weak with the intensity of the moment, she couldn't have turned the tables on him if she'd tried.

His hot lips stroked her collar-bone, pressing sweet kisses against the dip at her neck. Warm hands massaged her skin, making a path for his mouth to follow. The rasp of his tongue on her breast, the tug of his lips against her nipple made her arch into him, slick and ready and more than willing to do anything but wait to have him inside her body as deep as she felt him in her soul.

She slid her hands down his back, her fingers slipping over the silk of his boxers, gripping at his firm buttocks and remembering the power those muscles held to pound pleasure into her flesh. She pushed her pants over her hips and kicked them off the rest of the way to show him she was ready. Then peeled his boxers down his firm thighs.

His rigid penis pressed against her moist center as he wriggled his boxers off the rest of the way. But instead of plunging into her as she needed, he shifted to the side and continued his glorious attentions to her breasts, pushing them together so he could alternate his attentions and rapidly drive her insane.

Two could play this frustrating game. Now that she could think again, she reached for him, giving his penis a rough squeeze that made him groan, vibrating her nipple in his mouth. He was slippery from pressing against her, and she rubbed him appreciatively, wondering how much of this he could take. She was nearly out of her mind, and she'd come once already to take the edge off. Still, she'd never felt such a deep, aching desire before.

She pumped him quick and hard, stroking up and down. She knew she'd won the battle when he pulled her fingers off him and pinned her arms over her head.

Her mind whirling, her body on sensual overload, she nearly exploded when he slipped his hand between her legs, opening her so he could slide into her with one smooth thrust. She arched and screamed at the sensation, at once too much and not enough. Before she caught her breath his body began to undulate and rub against hers, his tempo increasing.

She stared up at the twinkling lights of the tree, her heart full of the loving act of bringing her fantasy to life. Moans echoed through the room until he covered her mouth with his, muffling the sounds while kissing her with a passion so wild and potent she felt proud to have elicited it from a man so controlled.

He possessed her body in a way he hadn't before, taking and giving at the same time. More alive than she'd ever felt, she wanted to touch every part of him. His lips on hers, their joining below, and her hands traveling every inch of his skin within reach. Her fingers slid over his back, slick with sweat, down to his buttocks, thrusting satisfaction into her body with fury.

Her body tightened around him and she gave into the climax she knew was building deep inside. Wrapping her legs around his back, she pulled him closer and surrendered to the pleasure he delivered.

She purred and panted as her body quaked around him, her head rolling from side to side. Her entire body shook, her inner muscles gripping him with each crest. She rode the waves of orgasm, her body slamming against his until he found his release.

The weight of his body was a comfort as he nuzzled against her neck. He slipped to the side, his breathing slowing until it kept pace with hers. Lauren smiled, enjoying every ripple of ecstasy still coursing through her body.

She turned, looking at his peaceful face, lost in obvious slumber. With a smile she leaned in and kissed the tip of his nose. When that got no response she stretched next to him, knowing sleep would come easy since the fire warmed the room. She tucked her body around his and dared to say what she'd wanted to all night, for a week really.

"I love you," she whispered, repeating the phrase over and over until she drifted off to sleep.

She loved him. Had said so every night this week when she'd thought he slept. But she hadn't mentioned a thing about it any other time. Not that they'd had much time together for a serious conversation. She was busy planning to expand her business and he was trying like hell to do the same.

With half of his investments in place, he needed to begin heavy fund-raising. Before, Anders had handled most of the recruiting of investors. But for Cameron to prove he could run the firm on his own, he couldn't ask for help. He had the limited partners lined up who would help mentor the companies through the start-up phase, but he needed more capital to grow the fund the way he'd outlined in the prospectus.

He had calls in to all of his targets, but he needed to nail down their interest. He was on track for the fund, but he wanted more time with Lauren before she opened her new store. Right now his workload would slow just as hers doubled.

His e-mail dinged, catching his attention. The name under the from label sent his pulse racing. Clive Braden was one of the richest men in the country, an impulsive investor known for seeking out longshots and making millions on them. He hated to be solicited, and so wasn't even on Cameron's wish list of possible investors. Until he opened the email.

With a six-hour layover between a flight from Tokyo

and a flight to Chicago tomorrow night, Braden wanted to discuss the alternative-energy fund. He'd heard the buzz from an investment banker who had passed along the prospectus. He gave the times of his flights and the email of his assistant to arrange a meeting.

Cameron leaned back in his chair. Just having Braden interested in his fund spoke volumes about its promise. If he convinced Braden to invest, he could close the fund to investors a month early at least.

His mind spun as he attacked his computer, polishing the prospectus with the latest details of the investments. He'd present the information casually, Lauren would work her magic making Braden feel comfortable, and his fund would be off and running at record speed. He might even be able to findsome time to break away before she opened her new store.

"You need to blink more." Lauren sauntered into his office, a vision in a plush velvet jacket so long it covered half of her jean-covered thighs and a white buttoned shirt she'd forgotten to button halfway up. She had the best clothes he'd ever seen.

"You look good."

"Why, thank you." She fluffed her gorgeous hair and gifted him with a spectacular smile. "Don't freak out."

Nothing good ever came after someone said those words. "What?"

"I was busy with the contractors, and didn't load my truck. So, I didn't bring turkey."

He eyed the white box that usually held his lunch. "What is it?"

"A chicken and spinach salad wrap. It's good, with bacon and apple and goat cheese.'

"Goat cheese?" She'd had him until she wanted him to eat something that came from a goat.

"You'll like it. It's like cream cheese with flavor. A cantaloupe strawberry salad and a new potato and pea salad. Apple cake too."

He warily unpacked, looking at the salads through the clear plastic containers. "Why are there onions in the fruit salad?"

"You'll like it, I promise. The cucumber and the melon are light and fresh, the strawberries sweet, the onion adds depth and the dressing tartness. It's a flavor explosion, I swear." She collapsed into the chair on the other side of his desk.

She looked so tired he decided the least he could do was try to eat the lunch. Maybe his good news would cheer her up.

"Have you heard of Clive Braden?"

"The name sounds familiar. Why?"

"He's interested in the renewable-energy fund."

"That's nice."

"Nice? Baby, he's one of the richest men in the country. It's not nice, it's career-making."

"Congratulations." She leaned forward in her chair, her elbows on her knees.

"Don't congratulate me yet. We have to convince him over dinner tomorrow."

"I can't do a dinner tomorrow. I have the vegan wedding to cater."

"Diego can handle that. How many people should we have? I'm thinking small so he doesn't feel pressured."

Lauren cleared her throat. "Diego isn't ready to do a wedding on his own. And not this wedding, anyway. Let's schedule it for another time."

Cameron shook his head. "He'll only be in town for six hours, assuming his flight is on time. I have maybe two hours here, Lauren. What time is the wedding?"

"Six-thirty. But I can't cater a sit-down dinner for two hundred and still make dinner for you."

"I need you there."

"I can't be there tomorrow night." She stood, crossing her arms over her chest.

"Fine. We'll hire another company to handle the wedding. I need you there. This is very important to me. To us."

Her mouth hung open, her eyes narrowing into slits. "Keeping my commitments is important to me. This is someone's wedding, Cameron. It's stressful enough without having your caterer drop you because her boyfriend wants her to come over. I won't do it."

"I need this, Lauren. We need this."

"No, *we* don't. Take them to a restaurant."

"You're not understanding how crucial this is. If I can bring in an investor like this, Anders will feel comfortable stepping down. I'll have control of the entire firm."

"From New York?"

"Yes." She closed her eyes and shook her head. Obviously not the right answer. "New York would mean less travel. You could move your business there."

"No, I couldn't cater parties in Seattle from Manhattan."

"Don't be so stubborn. Diego handles events every time we have a party that overlaps. He can handle this so that you can help me."

"What part of no aren't you comprehending?" She spoke slowly, anger evident on each word. "I can not have dinner with your client tomorrow. I have a wedding to cater. I need to make sure everything goes right for *my* clients. Clients who will still be with me after you go back to New York."

"That's not what I meant. I'm not going back to New York without you."

"Maybe you should, Cameron. Because I could never be with a man who doesn't respect my ambitions and expects me to morph into the perfect professional's wife when it suits him, but be too busy to notice how little I matter in his life the rest of the time."

She turned on her heel and marched from his office. He thought about chasing her, grabbing her by the shoulders and shaking some sense into her. She had a wedding to cater, which would be over and her menu forgotten in a few hours. His meeting could make their lives considerably more comfortable.

Damn her. Couldn't she see what they could accomplish together?

With a groan he took matters into his own hands. He typed "Seattle catering" into his web browser and called the first company that came on screen. He'd handle the party himself, and deal with her after he landed the biggest transaction of his career.

CHAPTER FIFTEEN

"WHAT is wrong with you?" Diego asked, stepping around Lauren in the corner of the hotel kitchen they were allowed to prepare the food in.

"Nothing is wrong with me." She continued to angrily jam guacamole into the cherry tomatoes. Damn weddings; always put her in a bad temper.

"Did you and Cameron have a fight?" Diego pulled out the egg-substitute mini frittatas and arranged them on a platter.

"Cameron is a jerk." Finished with her tomato platter, she started abusing mushroom caps, whacking them with artichoke and spinach filling. The wait staff came and went from the kitchen as quickly as possible, probably sensing her foul mood.

"What happened?" Diego stood next to her, his voice lowered below the buzz of the kitchen.

"He tells me yesterday afternoon that he needs me to cater a dinner for him tonight. And when I told him we were committed to a wedding, he expected me to change my plans. Actually suggested hiring another company to cater the wedding. This wedding, with the vegan everything. Can you imagine the nerve?"

"I told you I could handle this wedding on my own."

"That is not the point." She turned, whacking him square in the lapels of his chef's jacket with a hunk of spinach from her spoon.

"And the point is?"

"If he expects me to drop everything with no notice, just bail on my clients because he needs me, then he doesn't respect my career. That's not love, that's making life easier for him. And I work too damn hard to have someone treat what I do like a hobby."

"He said he needed you?"

"Like a broken record. But I can't live like that. I don't want to settle for someone who doesn't love me as much as I love him." If at all.

"How much does it weigh?"

"Excuse me?"

"You're putting it on a scale. So tell me, is it lighter than a feather, or heavier than a brick?"

"Very funny."

"I'm being serious. Men don't like to admit they need anyone, Lauren. He doesn't understand about poetic words and the right phrases you expect to hear. If a man wants to make you his, if he tells you he needs you, that's his definition of love. The word may elude him, but the feeling hasn't. That's all we're hardwired for. If a man says more, it's because a woman taught him to."

Lauren's heart sunk to the floor at how true Diego's words seemed. She'd dug in her heels because she thought if she gave in once, he'd always expect her to. Cameron had refused to bend in his insistence he needed her, but she saw it as him trying to break her desire to be successful.

She was being as petulant as him, refusing to give an

inch. When, really, she could compromise. Diego was more than capable of handling everything without her. And Nyla was here, micromanaging every detail of the wedding to precision.

"If he needs you, you should go."

"You're right." Lauren untied her apron.

Diego shuffled backwards, his hand over his heart. "Did the world just end? Did you actually admit I'm right?"

"Don't let it go to your head." On a new mission, Lauren gave one last set of instructions and hit the road. She knew they both needed to learn to give a little or things would never get better.

After a quick stop at her apartment to change, she re-hearsed her speech to him the whole drive to his house. But, arriving, she was surprised to see not a single car outside. Maybe he'd taken her advice and had the dinner at a restaurant.

She let herself in the kitchen door. Someone had been cooking in her kitchen, and they had left an awful mess. Ignoring the puzzling dirtiness for now, she walked further into the house, noting the baskets of rolls still on the table and empty bottles of wine. There had been a party here, but according to her watch it wasn't even eight.

"Cameron?" She called out, climbing the stairs and looking for answers. She found them huddled in his bathroom. "Are you okay?"

He shook his head slowly.

Cameron stopped throwing up long enough to fall asleep around three in the morning. To work out her frustrations, Lauren changed into a pair of his sweats and a T-shirt and scrubbed the kitchen.

She didn't know what made her angrier; that he'd replaced her as his caterer with so little thought, or that the company he'd used had given him food poisoning. A caterer was only as good as their last job, and this company would feel the repercussions if the other guests were as sick as Cameron. And if his investor got sick too, little chance of him signing on to the project remained.

Lauren felt guilty at first, but after having to bleach the kitchen and mop the floors her guilt had abated. Atonement by cleaning.

Exhausted, she climbed the stairs and crawled in bed next to him and slept until her cell phone started chiming downstairs. Trying not to wake Cameron, she sprinted to her phone, out of breath when she answered.

"Something funny is going on," Ricky said. "I just got here to start the breads, and there were four messages on the phone. Four cancellations for this week. And then before I could even get flour in the mixer, today's client called to cancel. Today's client!"

"Five cancellations already?" Her watch said it wasn't even eight in the morning. Something must have happened at the wedding after she'd left. She kicked her foot against the wall, then regretted it as she hopped around, trying to stop the pain.

"Actually six cancellations. One more after I tried to call Diego."

"I'll be there as soon as I can to try and figure this out." Try and throttle Diego was more like it. He should have called her last night if something had gone wrong. It would have started the troubleshooting process earlier.

After hanging up the phone Lauren looked down at her outfit. Cameron's clothes screamed walk of shame, but her dress would have been even more obvious. She'd simply tell everyone she'd been at the gym when Ricky had called. Maybe they'd believe she had really baggy workout clothes.

She went back upstairs to leave Cameron a note, but he was awake, sitting on the side of the bed and hanging his head. She sat next to him and ran a hand through his hair.

"Feeling better?"

"Marginally."

"I'm sorry you got sick."

"Me too. Braden showed up for thirty minutes, had some wine, asked two questions, and signed on to the project."

"Congratulations." He hadn't needed her after all. She really shouldn't have left the wedding.

"The caterer was awful. Rubbery food, and they didn't bring anything with them. No flowers, no music, no decorations. Nothing."

"I told you, that's a special service. It's not routine."

"I know. I just never realized all you put into a party. You make it look so easy."

"That's my job. And, speaking of my job, I need to get to work. There's something weird happening. Six cancellations already, including today's client. That never happens. Something must have gone wrong after I left the wedding last night."

"Something like what?"

"People getting sick, or the food not being prepared right, or the staff being rude."

"Sick, like I was sick?"

"Yeah, you can bet whomever catered last night won't be getting any business from the guests here, and anyone they know either."

Cameron fell back against the bed with a curse.

Lauren reached for him. "Do you need to be sick again?"

"You're going to kill me."

"Why would I do that?"

"Last night everyone wanted to know where you were, so I said you had a big wedding to cater. And then one of the wives said something about how you needed to be more dedicated to me and not your hobby and it annoyed me. So I said you made sure dinner was handled before you left because you wanted to make sure everything went perfectly."

Lauren hopped to her feet. "You told people Come For Dinner catered the poison party?"

"I thought I was helping."

"Helping who, Cam? Yourself?"

"No, helping you. You're always trying to impress the other wives."

"Never at the expense of my business! I've told you how careful I am about my parties, how much having my own business means to me. And now, because you acted like a spoiled brat and insisted on having a party when I couldn't be there and telling everyone I gave them food poisoning, my reputation is on the line. I can't believe you would sabotage my career!"

"I know you're upset, but I didn't do any of it to hurt you. I wouldn't do that."

"But you did hurt me, Cameron. After all I did to make sure your career was rosy—playing along with your fake girlfriend scheme and creating parties where you felt comfortable—this is how you repay me?"

"I'm sorry."

"You're sorry. Tell that to my wait staff who won't get a check this week because I don't have any work for them.

Tell that to my bank when I don't have enough money in my accounts to make payroll or pay the contractors."

"I'll pay for it."

"You can't throw money at this and make it go away. I don't want anything from you at all." She turned and marched down the stairs, grabbing her purse from the sparkling clean counter on her way out the door.

Cameron yelled after her to stop, but thanks to his food poisoning he wasn't fast enough to catch her.

Lauren hadn't returned a single one of his calls in the last five days. It gave him the perfect opportunity to announce the end to their fake relationship, and walk away unscathed. After everyone got sick, Anders wouldn't blame him a bit, might even leave him alone for a few months about replacing her with a new bauble.

But Cameron couldn't stand that he'd done something to hurt her, or her career. No matter what she thought, he liked that she knew who she was and how to take care of herself.

He had to convince her they had a future. He didn't want anything about their relationship to be fake; he wanted something as strong as she was. Strong enough to stand up to him and look out for them both.

Walking away now was impossible. And he couldn't let people believe Lauren had had anything to do with the food poisoning. An idea sparked in his mind to combine what she wanted and what he needed.

He dialed Come For Dinner, but, instead of asking for Lauren only to be told she was unavailable, he asked for Diego. And said a prayer that he could talk his way into a favor.

* * *

"I'm not going." Lauren stared at the spreadsheet covered in too much red on her computer screen.

"It's fifty people, Lauren. And most of our serving staff found other gigs this week. I need you there."

"It's a pity party, and everyone there knows it." And she hated to be pitied. Sure, Cameron had booked the party before the blowup, but she knew he kept up appearances for the sake of her business. A few weeks ago hosting a holiday bash with the richest in Seattle's social swirl had thrilled her, but now she knew everyone there would see through the ruse as quickly as she had. If she could afford to turn the party down, she would. But since half of their business for this week and next had evaporated, she had no choice.

Come For Dinner had to cater the party. But that didn't mean she had to be there. Serving appetizers to guests who would no doubt be whispering behind her back about the poison party and subsequent breakup.

"If you're there, you can explain to customers face to face. I agree it will sound like a cover-up over the phone, but in person you might be able to save us some business."

"I said no."

Lauren returned to her spreadsheet, wishing she could magically make the numbers change back to black. If things kept up this way she'd have to use the money for the new store just to keep the catering side afloat.

The phone rang next to her, and because she'd sent everyone but Diego home to save labor costs she had to answer it herself.

"Lauren, it's me. Don't hang up." Cameron's voice heated her in the wrong way. She needed to be angry, not relieved to hear his voice. She'd spent the week dodging his calls and deleting his voicemails without listening.

"I have nothing to say to you."

"I know you don't think so. But I need to see you in person. Come for dinner, tonight."

"I'm not interested in giving the gossips more carnage." Been there, done that, never letting them gnaw on her again.

"Please, I need to see you."

"I'm busy. Do you know what your disregard has done to my business?"

"I know. I want to make it right. I've—"

"You've done more than enough, Cameron. You got what you wanted. I'm sure the Anderses are off your back about a relationship, your funding is set so you can head back to New York, and you even get your perfectly understandable breakup. You have everything you want."

"I want you to love me." The line clicked off, leaving Lauren to stare at the phone in disbelief.

"Set up the Singapore slings on the entry table." Diego pushed the box into Lauren's hands and nearly shoved her out of the kitchen. She never would have selected the gaudy red cocktail, or the Asian theme of tonight's menu. But she wasn't in charge tonight, just kitchen help in a little black dress in case someone spotted her.

She didn't want to leave the kitchen tonight and risk having to explain what had happened to someone. But since the guests hadn't started to arrive yet, she did as Diego asked, surveying the setup for the party as she went.

In the living room was a large Christmas tree, professionally decorated with white ribbons and bows. Her heart panged, wondering if her twinkle-light tree still sat in the den.

Red and white was the theme of the night, from the candy canes on the napkins to the red and white poinsettias scattered on the table linens.

She set about making the pitchers of drinks, arranging everything so guests could easily help themselves. The doorbell rang behind her and she jumped. On autopilot Lauren sprinted to the stereo and pushed "play," acoustic Christmas carols filling the house as she answered the door. Bob and Sonja Anders. *Just perfect.*

They greeted her warmly, as if nothing had happened, and there was no way she was making the announcement. Fast on their heels more guests arrived. Lauren didn't even have time to look for Cameron as she greeted everyone; each guest seemed blissfully ignorant of the personal and professional pall hanging over her head.

The guest count rose to well over the fifty they'd expected. Without having to be told, her team moved furniture around to make more room for the guests. She swelled with pride at the team she'd created, hoping like hell she could do enough damage control tonight to keep them all employed.

The waiters milled about with egg rolls and sate, but few people tried them. Her heart ached at the sight.

"Smile, baby. It's your party." Lauren spun at the sound of her mother's voice, her eyes popping out of her head. Her mother looked fetching in her lavender slip dress and long flowing wrap. Her silver hair shined in the light.

"What are you doing here?"

"I was invited. Good thing I didn't give all my dresses to you." Lauren had sent out the invitations herself, hoping to tempt her mother out of the house. But that had been before everything had gone wrong, before only a morbid curiosity to learn what Cameron had meant on the phone had brought her to the party.

Tugging her elbow, Lauren pulled her mother past the foyer and dining room, into the den past the kitchen. What did you know—the twinkle tree was here, and sparkling.

"Mom, I told you, Cameron and I had a falling out. I explained everything to you—the wedding and the other caterer. I didn't expect you to still come tonight."

"Why not? You came."

"I'm working. We're short staffed."

"Playing hostess?"

"No. I'm in the kitchen."

Emma grinned. "In that dress?"

"In case someone sees me."

"Like when you're answering the door?"

Lauren groaned in frustration and pursed her lips together. It was one thing to risk abject humiliation by catering Cameron's party, quite another to have her mother watching.

"Baby, don't be angry so long life passes you by. You hate that I've done it, so don't make the same mistake."

"It's not the same thing. You lost a husband and a child, a whole life. You're allowed to be sad."

"They wouldn't have wanted me to put my life on hold for five years."

"No, but they would have understood."

"Do you?" Her mother's grassy green gaze peered through her.

"I do now. I didn't before."

"And you're willing to walk away from everything I'd give my life to have one more day with?"

"He doesn't want to be all that to me, Mom. And I can't settle for less. I need someone who understands why I have to have something besides my family, someone who knows that in my heart he'll come first even if he doesn't always on paper. I need to be more than someone's girl-friend, and he doesn't want that from me anyway."

"What do you see when you look in his eyes?"

Lauren's mind flashed to the time on the piano when she'd glimpsed behind his walls, to the time under the Christmas tree when he'd let her in so deep he'd made love to her soul. Her lips trembled with the flood of emotion, and she rolled them in, biting them down to keep from crying.

"Hold that thought." Emma kissed her cheek, disappear-ing into the hall.

Thankful for a moment alone to compose herself, Lauren sank down on the couch and let her heavy head fall into her hands. She didn't want to lose him, but she didn't want to lose herself either.

Footsteps tapped down the hall. Expecting her mother, Lauren looked up and gasped in shock. Cameron stepped into the room, his blue eyes made brighter by the French blue shirt he wore.

His lip curled in a mischievous grin. "You don't look like you are in the mood for a party."

"I've had a nasty week." She narrowed her eyes, won-dering what he was up to.

"I know. I've called everyone at the party and explained."

"You what! That will make me seem twice as guilty, as if I can't even take responsibility for my own mistakes."

"Not really. I talked to the husbands, not the wives. Men are simpler than women. They got it." He sat next to her on the couch. "We'll build your reputation back up, one party at a time."

"It's not just about the poison party, Cameron."

"You want me to be sorry for needing you?"

"No, I want you to be sorry for demanding I change my plans, then acting like a petulant child when I wouldn't."

"Is it really any more childish than only telling me you love me when you think I am asleep?"

Her eyes widened as she turned to stare at him. He did not just call her out when he should be apologizing! In turning to face him she got caught up in his stare, the bright blue gaze reaching inside of her to a place she'd vowed he would never touch again. But even if she locked that door, he had the key.

"I love you too. In a way that goes beyond affection, which was what I thought love was. I love you with a depth and a trust I never imagined possible. It tears me up that you think I'd hurt you on purpose, that you don't realize every hole in your soul is a hole in mine. I never wanted to need anyone. I tried to keep my distance to keep from hurting you, because I think I knew you loved me before you said the words. I didn't want to be responsible for disappointing you when I couldn't be all that you need."

"That's a cop-out. You can be anything you set your mind to." She tilted her chin to keep it from trembling. *He loved her.* The part of her that wanted to be the woman behind the man wrestled with the professional.

"I made a mistake out of anger, Lauren. Because I thought I couldn't trust you, trust anyone, until you showed me I already did. I'll make more mistakes, and so will you. I don't think any two people as strong willed as we are will be good at this right off."

"This?" She didn't know if she could trust his words, since they were exactly what she needed to hear.

"Us. You were right—we're terrible at dating. We should stop so that the next time we hit a bump, we both know there is no getting out of the car, unless it's to push."

"Maybe we just need regular maintenance so we don't break down." She giggled at matching his car analogy.

"You're right. Next time we have a row, we keep talking until we see a solution. When we disagree, too many people are affected. Think of all the poor folks who had to find second-rate caterers and won't have the holiday party they'd planned."

"Their loss for listening to gossips." She sat up straighter, actually feeling better. He had a point—clients would come back because Come For Dinner was good, better than their competition. And he had a point about them both lacking the best relationship communication skills.

"I need you, Lauren."

"Excuse me?" Her heart hiccupped. She had to know exactly what he needed her for.

Cameron knelt in front of her, his eyes glistening. "What I feel for you goes beyond wanting, Lauren. I need a woman who is my equal, who doesn't depend on me to fill up her life. I like that you know who you are, and you don't let that go for anyone, including me.

"I love you. And I've hated this last week. I hadn't realized how much I took for granted waking you up in the morning, or climbing into bed after you'd fallen asleep. Hated not having someone to talk to who didn't want anything more from me than a smile. I don't ever want to be without that again."

She felt the same way. Lauren smiled down at him, her thoughts dancing over the possibilities. He loved her, she loved him, and they both wanted to work this through, to make it more than either had thought they'd find.

"Let's try this for real. You and me together."

"Seattle or New York?" She couldn't move any time soon, not with all the effort her staff had put into the businesses, and the support her mother had given her ideas. Not for another two years at least.

"Wherever you are. I'd hate having to be away from you so much if we stayed here. But I could make it work. As long as we don't have kids before Anders steps down. Once I'm in control people will be willing to come to me. I don't want to miss a baby changing because they grow so fast."

"You want to have a baby?"

"Two." Her gaze met his and locked, staring until she felt herself melt into him, into the truth.

"I am only twenty-six."

"Then waiting is no problem."

She shook her head. He loved her, wanted to be with her, and wanted to have two babies with her, someday.

"This was the worst idea I have ever had."

"Excuse me?" She fisted his shirt, pulling him up to face her. She'd kill him. She'd taken self-defense classes. She'd use every move.

"I want nothing more than to spend the night showing you how much I love you, and we have a party going on outside that door. Do you think we can ditch our own party?"

Lauren thought of the tangle of people milling around the house. She didn't need to get caught up in it to celebrate. "I'm thinking we could have a private party, right here." She pulled him onto the couch with her.

Lying beside her, he kissed her as though her lips belonged to him. Just the way she liked it.

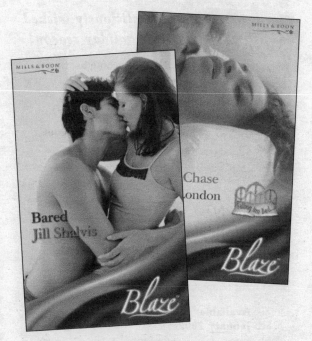